What Fire Dragons Treasure

DRAGON SHIFTERS OF ELYSIA BOOK FOUR

CRISTINA RAYNE

Fantastical Press

ALSO BY CRISTINA RAYNE

<u>Riverford Shifters</u>

Tempted by the Jaguar

Accepting the Jaguar

Rescued? by the Wolf

Tempted by the Tiger

Tempted by the—Lion?

Suspecting the Lioness *coming soon

<u>Elven King Series</u>

Shadows Beneath the Falling Snow (A Prequel Story)

Claimed by the Elven King

Date Night: A Bonus Short

Claimed by the Elven Brothers

<u>The Elven Realms</u>

(Sequel series to the Elven King series)

Memories of an Elven Prince

To Love an Elven Prince *coming soon

<u>Dragon Shifters of Elysia</u>

Where Sleeping Dragons Lie

When Fire Dragons Fall

What Stubborn Dragons Want

What Fire Dragons Treasure

Lords of the Vampire Underground

Tales from the Vampire Underground Collection

A Whisper in the Darkness *coming soon

Incarnations of Myth

Seeking the Oni

Falling for Enma *coming soon

Fractured Multiverse

(Writing as C.G. Garcia)

The Supreme Moment: Kairos

The Supreme Moment: Externus *coming soon

Black Crimson *coming soon

The Golden Mage Trilogy

The Kingdom of Eternal Sorrow

The Man Within the Temple

The Last Stone Cast

Dedicated to my family for always believing in me

The floorboards behind her creaked, and Amber Davis instantly froze in momentary terror, her heart nearly in her throat. One second, two, then a handful more, and she could suddenly breathe again when Garrett's expected angry growl didn't materialize. It had just been the house settling. Even so, that unexpected sound had spooked her enough to add as much speed as she dared to her hurried steps as she made her way on cat feet down the hall to her son, Matthew's, room.

It was true that Garrett slept like the dead whenever he passed out after one of his drinking binges, but that didn't at all guarantee that he wouldn't wake up if she made even the slightest sound. Amber had been waiting for this very opportunity for the past month, and she wasn't about to screw it up by waking him prematurely.

An image of Matty's wide, terrified eyes flashed in her mind, and Amber clenched her jaw angrily. No, she didn't dare wait any longer.

She had purposely left the door of her son's bedroom open wide enough for her to walk through sideways without touching when she had put him to bed that night, not wanting to risk the hinges squeaking. She had also put Matty to bed fully clothed and with a thin jacket and hood up to completely cover his blond locks as the nights had been a bit chilly that week.

Amber pulled out her cell phone to look at the time. 2:00 a.m. Good. She still had thirty minutes to get to the designated street corner a few blocks away.

After putting the cell phone on Matty's nightstand, she dropped to her knees and felt under his bed for the backpack she had hidden there only just today. She slipped it on and then turned to her sleeping son. Her heart clenched at the sight. He looked like a doll sprawled out with one hand fisted up near his head and his blankets bunched up around his feet.

As carefully as she could, Amber scooped him up into her arms and slowly positioned him until his little head rested on her shoulder. She was relieved when his only reaction to being disturbed was a single, heavy sigh. She prayed with everything she had in her that he wouldn't wake up. At three years old, Matty was currently at the stage of asking endless questions and would likely not understand their need for silence.

Her eyes fell on the stuffed T-rex lying against his pillow. It was his favorite. Despite the risk of jostling him awake, Amber bent to snatch it up. He would need something familiar and beloved to comfort him during the uncertain days ahead.

Despite all her caution, it seemed the floorboards creaked horrifyingly loud with every step she took, as though the damned house was just as determined as her husband to keep her and Matty prisoners within. It was a wonder she hadn't had a heart attack from the anxiety by the time she made it out the back door.

The night was still and quiet, the only sounds her anxious breathing and the crunch of leaves beneath her feet as Amber hurried across the backyard to the gate that opened into an alley. That the expected bellowing of her husband never materialized behind her only served to feed the huge knot of fear that was painfully making it difficult to breathe.

She couldn't fail here. She *couldn't*.

A renewed sense of determination injected speed into her legs as she sped-walked as fast as she dared down the dark alley, mindful of waking Matty. A child talking loudly at this ungodly hour would be remembered if any of their neighbors happened to be awake. She would leave the bastard no clues if at all possible.

Luckily for her heart, no cars moved down the neighborhood streets as Amber hurried down shadowy sidewalks, or miracle upon miracles, no barking dogs to announce their passage. She had never realized just how quiet her neighborhood was until that night.

Small favors. Maybe the Fates weren't quite the assholes she always thought them to be.

By the time Amber made it to the corner house a few blocks north of her own house that her friend, Keri, had designated to the rideshare app for pickup, Matty seemed to have gained twenty pounds even with all the excess adrenaline wreaking havoc throughout her body. The house was completely dark inside, a dim porchlight its only illumination. The property was currently empty and wouldn't appear on the market for at least another week according to Keri. Most importantly, the house was in no way connected to her or Keri as the place wasn't being sold by the real estate firm Keri worked for.

Amber hurried up the stone porch steps to sit on the small, wooden porch swing located off to the side just out of the porch light's reach. She wanted to give the impression that she had been waiting for her ride for longer than a few minutes.

Despite finally able to rest a bit, her heart refused to slow down. Even though it was likely that her husband was still passed out in their bedroom, Amber still felt like a doe with hunting dogs snapping at her heels. At least Matty was still blissfully asleep and unaware of just how much his world was about to change. His soft exhales against the clammy skin of her neck were warm and soothing. Right now, his obliviousness was the most important thing.

It was too dark to see the face of her wristwatch properly, and Amber had, of course, left her phone behind. She didn't want to risk waking Matty by standing to move closer to the light to see the time. All she could do was sit on that swing trembling with anxiety and pray that she hadn't missed her ride.

This was it. This was her last shot to save her son from that monster, and it made her sick to even think she might have already failed.

Headlights appeared at the end of the block, and Amber instantly stiffened in alert, her already racing heart increasing with a painful lurch. She watched the vehicle—a car—approach at a slow speed with narrowed eyes. Her arms unconsciously hugged her son more tightly against her chest.

Even though she expected it, when the dark-colored car stopped in front of the empty house, the knot of tension in her chest tightened.

It's okay. It's okay. It isn't *him. It's just the rideshare.*

Amber recited those reassuring words over and over like a mantra right up until she was close enough to see that the driver was a young blonde woman and not one of the usual goons that Garrett's family employed for security.

"Thank you so much, and sorry to call for a ride so late," Amber said as she carefully, but awkwardly, climbed into the backseat of the car. "Having car trouble at the last minute really is the worst, but I really didn't want my mom out driving at this hour."

"No problem. I can always use the extra cash," the young woman said with a shrug and a friendly smile.

The radio was playing at a fairly low volume, but after glancing at Matty, her driver turned off the radio altogether.

"Nurse?" the driver asked.

Amber smiled. "Yes. Today's an early shift, unfortunately."

A complete lie, but given the odd hour, she had dressed in a pair of scrubs, a pair of wire-rimmed glasses, and a wig of long, auburn curls as part of her cover, not only for anyone who might recognize her, but also for her driver. A quick glance down confirmed that none of Matty's hair was peeking out from under his hood.

Given her comment about her mom and that Keri had instructed her rideshare to drop her off at a second vacant residence clear across town, a working mom and her son would be less likely to stand out in her driver's mind.

Once her husband woke and realized they were gone, she had no doubt that Garrett would have every cell phone in the state screeching with—ironically—an Amber Alert for their son. Threatening her with charges of kidnapping was one of the asshole's favorite threats ever since the first time Amber had tried to leave him back when Matty had only been six months old.

Hopefully, they would be long gone from the city when that inevitability happened.

Amber was relieved when her driver didn't try to chat once they were moving, probably not wanting to wake up Matty. The less she had to say to this woman, the smaller the chance that Amber would trip herself up.

Still, she couldn't quite relax enough to slow her heartbeat. She really needed to calm down. The last thing she needed was to faint in either the car or out on the street somewhere before she could even reach the next step in her escape plan because her anxiety was shooting her blood pressure through the roof.

What felt like hours later when in actuality it was probably no more than fifteen minutes, they pulled up in front of a brick home that was completely dark. Amber's eyes did a quick sweep out of all the windows in search of people as she unfastened her seatbelt, but thankfully, she detected no movement among the homes on either side of the street.

"Hopefully, your day's better from here on out," her driver said sympathetically as Amber opened the door as quietly as she could.

"Thanks, and have a good night, too," Amber replied quietly.

Matty still didn't utter so much as a peep as she awkwardly slid out of the car. She slowly headed towards the empty house's front walk, relieved beyond measure when her rideshare drove off instead of politely waiting for them to make it into the house.

Once the car was out of sight, Amber turned and headed for the driveway that stretched a bit beyond the back of the house where a black, older model Honda sedan sat waiting for them as planned. A feeling as though she had just found the pot of gold at the end of the rainbow when she hadn't really believed it would ever happen washed through her, nearly making her dizzy with euphoria.

It was finally going to happen! She and Matty were finally getting out from under that bastard's thumb!

Amber had Matty strapped into the car seat in the back in record time, his T-rex plushie tucked securely into his side. The giddiness of escape didn't leave her until they had made it out of Houston. With only the blackness of the highway ahead and her own racing thoughts as her companions, her earlier anxiety began to creep back in.

She had made it out of the city unmolested, yes, but they were still hours away from what she desperately hoped would be their final destination—North Point, Texas.

A folded sheet of paper tucked between the passenger seat and the center console abruptly caught her eye. Amber reached for it without taking her eyes from the road. Unfolding it one-handed, Keri's messy handwriting immediately jumped out. Her friend's message was short, and heartbreakingly to the point:

The burner phone you asked me to get you is in the glove compartment. Good luck and stay safe! Give Matty lots of hugs and kisses from me, and I hope to God to see you both again someday, happy and whole.

Amber's eyes tightened and her heart clenched painfully, but the sudden memory that flashed through her mind's eye of blood dripping from Matty's mouth had her gritting her teeth in determination and anger instead of giving in to the tears that had been threatening all day.

Never again.

CHAPTER TWO

It wasn't her imagination.

Amber had seen that silver sedan behind her back in San Antonio and again in Temple. Both times, it had been at least four cars behind her and too far away to get a good look at its driver and passengers in her rearview mirror.

Her pulse sped up. It might just be paranoia. She desperately *hoped* that's all it was, but "better safe than sorry" had become her mantra ever since she had bundled Matty up in his jacket and set out into the dead of night.

Maybe I should've gone north to Lufkin or College Station after all... she fretted.

But no—the whole point of taking I-10 to San Antonio was to leave a false clue in the small chance that someone would remember her, make it seem as though she were heading for Laredo to cross into Mexico. She had made a point to take both their passports as well as Garrett's, a feat that had only been possible because of the asshole's insufferable arrogance in thinking that he had her completely cowed after that terrible night a couple of months ago.

He had left all three passports in the same unlocked desk drawer in his home office where they had sat since their foray into Mexico last summer, no doubt to taunt her. Hell, he hadn't even bothered to lock his office door even though he always had at the beginning of their marriage. That very fact, that lack of trust, should have been a red flag, but Amber was the first to admit that she had been a naïve idiot from the moment she had met him during her freshman year of college to the first days of their marriage.

Her attention moved from the silver sedan in her rearview mirror to Matty. He was currently happily paging through one of his favorite picture books—a physical book—and munching on an animal cracker. Given the long drive they still had ahead of them, Amber regretted leaving his tablet behind. However, she hadn't dared to bring anything electronic that could be tracked. She had only dared to activate her prepaid phone once she had left San Antonio and only because she had needed to use a map app to find a route to the city of Temple off the interstate.

Her attention briefly focused once more on the silver car in the rearview mirror that was *still* four cars back. Had turning on the phone been a major mistake after all? Should she have picked a more obscure route? At this point, she couldn't afford even a tiny mistake!

Amber had been planning on stopping to pick up lunch from a fast food drive-through in Waco and just eat in the car, but if the silver car continued to follow her while within Waco's city limits, then she would just try to lose it—hopefully without getting lost herself—before heading north again. The fruit cups, juice boxes, and other snacks she had packed for the long journey would tide Matty over until they reached Dallas.

But what if that silver car does *seem to be following you?* An invisible hand painfully squeezed her heart. *That would mean—*

No. She couldn't even think it.

This is going to work, dammit!

In truth, Amber didn't want to think about the last, most important requirement for her plan to work. True, if it did work, it would be the best-case scenario in her current situation, the one she wholeheartedly felt was best for Matty, but deep down, she knew it was a long-shot. She, of course, had a Plan B and even a Plan C in case her Plan A crashed and burned, but having to go with one of the latter two would be crushing.

There was only one place on Earth that Amber felt Matty would be safe from Garrett and his despicable father, the senator, if all the research she had done was even a quarter true.

Elysia South.

Not even Senator Henry Johnson could penetrate the energy shield that had surrounded Elysia South since the day the dragon kingdoms had appeared across the world seemingly out of thin air.

For over a year, Amber had heard whispers about humans, especially battered women, being granted a form of sanctuary—at least temporarily—by the dragons by pleading their case to one of the dragons' border guards. Normally, Amber would have scoffed at such a claim, but it was a fact that one of their princesses was a human from Earth. How that had happened was a mystery that no one seemed to have an answer for, not even Garrett's father who was a powerful US senator.

Amber was extremely curious about the answer herself, but when she had watched that documentary about all things Draknos last year, what had caught her attention was President Mitchell's praise of Princess Briana's kindness, diplomacy, and hope that one day humans and dragons could live freely together all over the globe as well as in the four Elysia kingdoms. If that was the dragons' sincere wish, then the whispers of sanctuary held more weight for her.

"Mommy?" Matty abruptly asked.

"Yes sweetie?"

"When are we going to see the dragons?"

"Soon, sweetie," Amber promised. "The dragons just live really far away from our house."

Even if the sanctuary rumor turned out to be false, at the very least, she could keep her promise to her little boy of seeing a real live dragon up close thanks to the handful of dragon-viewing platforms set up just last year around the perimeter of the energy shield that were open to the public.

"Can we get chicken nuggets, too?" he asked.

They were only about five minutes from Waco, and the silver car was still several cars behind them. She hoped to God that the damned car turned out to be a huge nothing burger. Aside from the obvious, Amber hated the thought of making Matty wait for a full meal, especially when he really couldn't understand why they had to.

"In a bit," Amber forced herself to say cheerfully.

Seemingly satisfied, Matty's attention went back to his book, but Amber couldn't relax. Not until that silver car was gone from her sight.

Her heart was in her throat when she turned off the highway at the Waco exit, praying with everything in her that the silver car wouldn't follow. It was only when the four cars, as well as the worrisome silver one, passed the exit that Amber noticed that she gripped the steering wheel so tightly that her knuckles had turned white and her fingers were starting to hurt.

God—if she didn't relax and get out of her own head, she was going to have a nervous breakdown before they even hit Dallas. She couldn't keep Matty safe if she were a freaking mess.

Amber concentrated on breathing more slowly and getting her heartrate down, but no matter how much she scolded herself that the silver car had just been a false alarm, she couldn't quite make herself stop from scanning all the vehicles in her immediate area for that familiar silver as she drove around Waco aimlessly for the next twenty minutes.

Once she was satisfied that no one appeared to be following them, Amber consulted her maps app for the nearest fast food restaurant that served chicken nuggets while waiting at a stop sign within a residential area, happy that Matty wouldn't have to wait to eat lunch after all. After going through the drive-through, she paused in the restaurant's parking lot just long enough to open and spread out Matty's food and drink on the tray attached to his car seat.

On her way out of Waco, Amber nearly had a heart attack when a silver car suddenly appeared behind her right before she took the onramp to the interstate, but on a second look, it wasn't the same car. They were halfway to Dallas by the time she was able to settle her racing heart to something less panicky.

The fact that they were making good time and would likely make it to North Point well before dark allowed Amber to settle down even more. It was likely that she would be able to make it to one of North Point's dragon-viewing platforms today. Matty could even be *safe* tonight.

The thought made Amber's eyes well up with tears.

Maybe she wasn't a complete failure as a mom after all...

CHAPTER THREE

"Are we going to see the dragons now?" Matty asked, this time a little more impatiently.

"Yep," Amber replied, trying to keep her sudden nerves out of her voice.

Given the past year of violence Matty had witnessed at home, he was exceptionally sensitive to warbles or stress in her voice. Such changes in her tone instantly triggered fear in her son, and damned if she would make him feel anything but excitement today, especially by accident.

"See that sign up ahead? It says "NP-2 Dragon-Viewing Platform.""

Matty was suddenly leaning so far forward that had he not been strapped in, he would have fallen out of his car seat. "Where? Where? I don't see them, Mommy!"

Amber forced a laugh. "You won't be able to see them just yet, sweetie. We're still too far away."

Please God let us see one today...

"Can I ride the dragons?" he asked excitedly.

"Dragons aren't ponies, Matty, but mommy *is* going to try to talk to one."

Matty's eyes widened. "Dragons *talk!*"

"These dragons do. They can also—well, you'll see," Amber hedged. It probably wasn't such a good idea to bring up the shapeshifting thing. Sure, Matty was bright for a little boy just shy of four, but the concept of dragon-shifters would probably only confuse him unnecessarily.

They were currently traveling north on a county road that ran parallel to North Point's eastern city limits and dead ended at Elysia South's energy shield. One of the most popular dragon-viewing platforms was located just off that road about a couple of hundred yards from the energy shield. All the popular dragon online fan sites had agreed that the NP-2 platform saw the most dragon activity daily out of the three that surrounded Elysia South.

Fans speculated that it was because the dragons that patrolled that stretch of shield were the friendliest out of the bunch. Amber certainly hoped so—no, she *counted* on it.

Amber saw the red and black dragon landing in the distance the same time Matty squealed in delight, "Look, Mommy! A dragon! Look! Look!"

Although she knew from the countless videos she had watched of the energy shield surrounding Elysia South, it was still a shock to see such a mythical creature land so gracefully a few hundred yards to the right of where the road ended in what looked like an open field without any visible barriers between them. The energy shield was invisible unless it was disturbed—she had seen all the videos on various social media platforms of idiots throwing everything from rocks to bowling balls to various liquids at the shield in the hope for clicks. Only when it was disturbed could you see something like ripples of light race through the air.

Eager to see the awe and delight light up her son's face, Amber's eyes flickered to the rearview mirror. "I see the dragon, sweet—"

She choked on the rest of the endearment as Amber saw a silver car about a mile behind her speeding right for them.

No, no, no! This can't be happening right now! Not when we're so close!

Now completely panicked, Amber floored the accelerator. The county road was the only way in and out of the area. She had no doubt that whoever was in the car would either try to run her off the road or, if she managed to turn around in the visitor parking lot up ahead, follow her until the car ran out of gas.

If you ever try to leave me again, to take my son from me, I'll make sure it's the last thing you do. I will not *be humiliated!*

Garrett's menacing voice surfaced among her frantic thoughts. Was Garrett in that silver car? Had he been following them since they had left the house, taunting her by allowing her to believe that she had managed to get away?

Amber didn't dare take her eyes off the road to look in the rearview mirror for confirmation. She *had* to get to that shield no matter what!

"M-mommy?" Matty asked in a shaky, soft voice.

Her heart broke. There it was, the fear she had hoped to never hear in Matty's voice again. Her unconscious body language had likely damned her more than her aborted reply.

"We're going to talk to that dragon, sweetie," Amber replied resolutely, relieved that her voice remained firm. "Mommy's just going to drive on the grass now, so the ride might get a bit bumpy."

All the reliable information she had been able to find about all the dragons seen from the various viewing platforms stated that that they were guards patrolling the perimeter of their kingdom. Surely the dragon she was currently careening towards would see that she was in trouble and help her, right? Or would the dragon perceive her as a threat?

A loud series of pops sounded behind them. The steering wheel lurched along with the front of the car, and for a terrifying split-second, Amber thought the car was about to flip over. By a sheer miracle, she managed to fight her first instinct to slam on the breaks and instead, take her foot off the gas pedal. She tightened her grip on the steering wheel and fought to take back control of the car as it slowed.

What the hell had happened? Had she blown a tire? Amber started to panic anew at the thought, but then the terrified sob behind her stopped her panic cold. No —she couldn't freak out now.

"It's okay, Matty. It's okay," she crooned thickly. "Mommy's going to stop the car, and we'll go outside to see the dragon."

The car had slowed down enough that she felt she could safely tap the brakes now. As the car came to a stop, she caught a glimpse of the silver car still barreling towards them. Shit! She had possibly a minute, tops, to get Matty out of the car before Garrett or whoever the bastards were in the car were upon them. She wouldn't put it past them to try to run her down before she could get Matty out of the car.

She jumped outside and tugged open the back door within seconds. Matty was crying in soft gasps, one little fist stuffed into his mouth as though he were trying to stifle the sound. His other hand gripped his dinosaur plushie so tightly that his little fist shook. Amber cursed again as she frantically undid the straps with fingers that suddenly seemed too fat and clumsy, her own breaths coming in short, panicked gasps.

Then Matty was in her arms, and she ran as fast as she could towards the energy shield before her brain fully registered the action. Another loud pop sounded behind her, then another, and it was only then that Amber finally understood what the sound was.

Someone is freaking shooting *at us!*

They were finally close enough to the energy shield to see that the dragon was seated on his or her haunches, head turned towards Amber and Matty as she desperately tried to make her legs run faster.

"Help me!" Amber screamed as loud as she could.

They were almost there! She was finally close enough to see the dragon's enormous, fire-colored eyes staring intently in their direction.

Another loud pop rang out, and she choked on a half cry, half gasp as her right calf erupted in fire. Her leg instantly crumpled. She barely managed to twist to the side and avoid landing on Matty as she slammed hard, side-first, into the ground in an uncontrolled skid.

"Help...me! *P-please!*" Amber cried desperately, gasping after the breath that had been knocked out of her.

She could hear men shouting behind her, but she couldn't make out any words over the sound of her own heart beating frantically in her ears and Matty's crying.

"They're trying...to kill...me!" she wheezed. "They're trying...to take...my son! Sanc...tuary...we need...!"

Amber tried to pull herself up onto her knees, but she couldn't quite get enough breath for the effort. They were going to catch them! The bastard that had shot her would probably leave her to bleed out in the dirt and take Matty! She couldn't allow—she couldn't—

Darkness suddenly clouded her sight, and for one anguished breath, Amber thought she was losing consciousness. However, a wash of warm air abruptly engulfed her a split-second before something hard and just as warm wrapped around her body, pressing both Matty and his plushie more snuggly against her chest. It was only when she realized that her body had been lifted from the ground and the ground also started to move that she understood what must have happened.

Her arms instinctually tightened around Matty, and

Amber stilled completely. More gunfire sounded, but she heard it as though from a TV playing in a distant room.

"*Shh*, it's okay, Matty. It's okay," Amber soothed breathily, her lungs still not recovered from her fall.

She felt Matty's hands grip her shirt more tightly, but at least his sobs were calming. She prayed that he hadn't seen her bleeding. Her leg didn't hurt at all, but she knew better. If they hadn't been surrounded by warmth, she would likely have been cold and trembling from shock. The pain would definitely come later and with a vengeance.

"Don't move," a booming, deep and accented voice said from above as the darkness increased around them. "I must fly us to another location. You're safe within my hands."

Safe...

"You see, Matty," Amber whispered into his ear, "the nice dragon helped us and is going to take us for a ride in the sky."

Matty's breaths were still coming in short, half-sobs, and she feared that he was too lost in his fear to really hear her. Those bastards! That complete *asshole!* Whether Garrett had been in the silver car or not, someone in that car had shot at them. Never mind her, but they could have hit Matty! What kind of sick bastard would shoot at someone carrying a toddler?

They had probably shot out her tires, too! It made her sick to think about how the car had nearly rolled. She had been going at least eighty. At that speed, both she and Matty could have been killed if she hadn't gotten the car back under control.

As Amber shook and raged in her mind, her stomach abruptly dropped amidst the sound of wings flapping and a bit of jostling against the hard surface at her back. Scales? She couldn't be sure. Matty gasped and pressed his face into her chest, likely feeling the abrupt change of elevation as well.

She took a moment to breathe deeply and try to calm herself, although in the back of her mind, she worried about the bleeding wound on her leg. The dragon had been watching her run towards the shield when she had been shot. Surely, he knew just how fragile humans were given that at least one human lived among them for sure.

Amber couldn't bear the thought of passing out from blood loss and leaving Matty terrified among strangers, especially a dragon. Seeing dragons flying around on his tablet or on TV was one thing. Realizing just how big they were in real life and that one had you in its grip was another. This was likely one of the worst ways to introduce a child to a dragon, but at least he hadn't seen one of them roast anyone or even roar. The dragons of Elysia South were firedrakes after all...

We made it into Elysia South!

The disbelief in that thought, that her whole improbable, crazy plan had actually worked, and they were now soaring across the sky clutched within the hands of a real-life dragon made Amber almost break out into hysterical giggles. It was absurd! It was glorious! It made Amber doubly terrified now of what was to become of them.

When had things in her life ever gone according to plan?

Her marriage, she had thought, once upon a time.

But we all know how that turned out, don't you? Amber thought bitterly.

She just hoped for once this time would be different, for Matty's sake. They were finally in a place where Garrett's family couldn't reach them, and she would get down on her knees and beg until her knees bled and her voice gave out if that's what it took to keep it that way.

CHAPTER FOUR

It seemed to take both an eternity and no time at all before Amber felt her stomach drop again. A few seconds later, the impact as the dragon landed reverberated strongly throughout her body. She had spent the time in the semi-darkness of their warm cocoon whispering reassurances to Matty and mentally fretting about how she was going to convince the dragon to let them stay.

Amber winced and scrunched her eyes shut when the hand that had been covering them was suddenly removed, and the normal brightness of the day hit her eyes. She then slowly cracked her eyes open, allowing her eyes to gradually adjust for a few seconds before she squinted up at their savior.

Had Amber not known that the saurian creature

looking down at her with bright, orange-colored and vertically-pupiled eyes that didn't seem to blink was a talking, sentient being that was sometimes a man, she might have screamed in terror.

Instead, she pushed herself up by her elbow, then with a bit more difficulty, to a sitting position using one of her hands as she clutched Matty protectively with the other. That was slightly better. At least this way, she didn't feel like a mouse staring up at the gullet of the snake about to swallow her whole. Much.

Amber swallowed thickly, her mouth suddenly irritatingly dry. "Thank you so much—for saving us from those thugs."

"You're injured—bleeding." The dragon frowned, his nostrils flaring, before he carefully lowered them onto the thick grass before she could even open her mouth to reply. "My questions can wait. Is the child injured, as well?"

Mentally, for sure, Amber thought in despair. Aloud, she replied, "I don't think so. He's just terrified right now."

The dragon's frown deepened. "Perhaps if he saw me as just a man..."

Huh? Wait—was he going to—!

"No, no," Amber said hastily as the dragon took a single step back. "That's not why—"

She nearly swallowed her tongue as the red and black dragon began to rapidly shrink, twist, and shift his form like some kind of wild and disturbing morphing effect gone wrong. Then her face nearly spontaneously combusted as seemingly, between one blink and the next, a tall, dark-haired and *naked* man with muscles that went on for miles now stood before her. He stared down at her with narrowed eyes, the same fiery orange as the dragon's had been, set in a startlingly handsome face with day-old stubble.

Amber knew she should look away, that it was likely rude to stare. The last thing she needed to do was cause this incredible being offense before she could even plead her case, but the moment those unusual eyes caught her gaze, it was as though her body had been ensnared and frozen within a piece of her namesake.

"My son wasn't—wasn't scared of *you*," she blurted out, wincing internally at how desperate she sounded. "He loves dragons and dinosaurs, and..." Her voice trailed off in embarrassment as the man's lips curved up in obvious amusement.

"So I see," the once dragon said as he gestured down at her with his chin.

Amber's eyes immediately looked down at Matty. She relaxed minutely. Oh, the plushie. She caught an inadvertent glimpse of his entire exposed front as she looked back at him before she quickly looked up at his face. She could feel her cheeks burn even hotter than before. He definitely was all human male now, magnificently so...

The dragon-man knelt beside her without further comment or even a hint of self-consciousness about his nudity and gestured at her right leg. "May I examine your wound?"

"Oh, yes, of c-course," she stammered, flustered beyond belief.

"I'm Raphek of the House of the Red Flame. What's your name?" he asked as fingers that were a lot warmer than a regular person's should be carefully wiped some of the blood away from a wound that was thankfully smaller than she had feared.

Had those goons used a high-powered rifle, they could have blown her entire lower leg off.

"Amber. Amber Davis," she answered, wincing at the sudden flair of pain despite his careful touch.

"Like the earth gem?" he remarked without taking his eyes off his hands as they probed the gunshot wound.

"Yes—*ow!*" The dragon-man had slightly dug his pinkie finger into the wound.

"Sorry." He sighed. "It's as I feared. The bullet is still lodged within your muscle, though luckily it missed any major arteries. I don't suppose you have a handkerchief or something that I can use to temporarily bind your wound until I can get you looked at by a proper healer?"

She shook her head. In her haste to reach the energy shield, she had been forced to leave her backpack with all the extras she had packed behind in the car. They were now literally left with only the clothes on their back.

ID, passports, money, all of it—lost...

Undeterred, her rescuer proceeded to rip off a piece of her jeans starting just below the knee of her injured leg as easily as though the denim were made of tissue paper.

"And the little one? What's his name?" the dragon-man asked as he carefully wrapped the piece of denim tightly around her calf.

"Matthew," Amber replied through gritted teeth. Apparently, her initial shock had worn off enough for her to feel every inch of the bullet wound. "But most everyone calls him Matty."

The dragon-man's attention shifted to her son. "Hello, Matty," he greeted with a gentle smile. "My name is Raphek."

At the mention of his own name, Matty turned his head slightly and peeked up at the dragon-man for a couple of seconds before bashfully hiding his face in her shirt again. "Hello," Matty replied, so softly that Amber almost didn't hear him.

"You have no idea how nice it is to meet you, Raphek," Amber said sincerely.

After tying off her new makeshift bandage, Raphek sat down, cross-legged next to her. "I have never seen two humans attacked in such a manner outside of one of your movies," he said grimly.

Amber stiffened. Right. Time for the interrogation.

"While I can't be a hundred percent sure of the identities of those men chasing after us," Amber said slowly, "I can't think of anyone else except Matty's father or grandfather who would send those kinds of thugs after us. For all I know, Garrett—Matty's father—was among them, but I wasn't about to stop and look at them once I had gotten out of my car."

"Were they trying to kill you?" His voice positively dripped with disgust.

"Me? Undoubtably."

"Why?"

Amber could barely get the words out around the huge knot of despair that had suddenly formed in her throat. "Because he wants to take Matty away from me. Because he would rather kill me than have what would likely be a nasty custody battle 'stain his reputation and ruin his chances to become a senator or even president' someday."

She wasn't sure dragons even knew what custody battles were or even divorce, but a quick glance at Raphek's face showed her that he understood enough.

"To take a child away from his mother is beyond despicable," Raphek growled. "You said a word—sanc-something-or-other—when you bled upon the ground and pleaded for my help. I didn't understand it."

Amber's heart sank. "Sanctuary. Is that not the right word? Or—" She paused. No, she couldn't afford not to tell him at least some of the truth. "I heard rumors of the Draknos helping human women stay safe from their abusive spouses. Matty's father's family is powerful. Both politically and financially. After Garrett became verbally abusive and then physically violent with me, I tried to leave him, but he threatened to ruin my parents' business if I didn't go back to him. For any other man, that would have been just bluster, but not for that family. They're an old, dynastic family that made their fortune in oil. Garrett's father, Henry, is especially well-connected. Then after Matty was born…"

She trailed off and pressed her lips together tightly to stave off the sob that wanted to burst from deep within her. Dammit! She wouldn't cry! Not here. Not in front of this dragon-man that she didn't even know.

"You are asking for asylum," Raphek said slowly, the look in his eyes undecipherable as he scrutinized her own.

"Yes. Asylum," Amber agreed, a desperate note in her tone no matter how hard she tried to hide it.

Asylum didn't quite fit her situation, but it was close enough to what they needed from Elysia South that she didn't dare correct him.

Amber squared her shoulders and then looked him dead in his uncanny eyes. "Elysia South is the one place Henry can't step foot in. I came to this particular dragon-viewing platform in the hope of seeing a dragon —sentry?—that I could plead for asylum from the man that is a danger to my son and me. I left Houston early this morning. I never expected Garrett's thugs to find me so soon or to open fire in front of witnesses. I saw a bunch of cars parked in the viewing platform's parking lot before I was forced off the road, so there had to be at least a handful."

Raphek's eyes seemed to literally ignite with fire. "This man, Garrett, he's hurt the child before?"

Amber's arms once again tightened around Matty. "The bastard backhanded Matty hard across the mouth and made him bleed quite badly. I knew in that horrible moment that no matter what happened to me, I had to get Matty far away from him and that family permanently. Elysia South is the only place on this earth that I believe Matty will be safe from that monster."

"Far be it for me or any Draknos to turn away a child in need," Raphek said gruffly. He abruptly stood, and Amber once again hastily averted her eyes before she could get another inadvertent eyeful of his manhood. "I must speak with my captain in the Guard as well as the king. In the meantime, allow me to fly you both to stay with a couple of friends that live within the mountain. They will call for a healer to see to your wound properly while I am occupied."

"I don't want to inconvenience anyone..." Amber said uncomfortably. The last thing she wanted was to intrude in someone's home.

"My friend's mate, Emma, will understand your plight better than you think," Raphek interjected with the same kind tone he had used while talking to Matty. "She's only one of two humans that live here perma-nently in Elysia South."

Amber sucked in a sharp breath as the mountain of problems that were currently riding on her shoulders lifted just enough for her to breathe a bit more easily. Even if only a couple, there really were humans living among these dragon-shifters. Maybe her whole crazy plan wouldn't turn out to be such a fool's errand after all.

"Matty and I would love to meet them," Amber said sincerely.

Matty lifted his head and looked up at her with wide eyes still wet with tears. "Are we going to ride the dragon now?"

Amber's smile was more a grimace. Yikes. She really needed to make him understand that the dragons were people not animals sooner rather than later.

"No sweetie. We're going to sit on his hand while he flies just like before."

Matty tilted his head quizzically. "But where's the dragon?"

"Right here, little one," the same deep, dragon voice from earlier abruptly announced.

Amber's gaze shot up from Matty's face, startled. Sure enough, the red and black dragon from before had replaced Raphek's human form.

To Amber's surprise, Matty's lips stretched into a wide smile. "He's so big, Mommy!"

No matter how much he seemed to love dragons and dinosaurs, she had honestly expected him to be scared— or at the very least, nervous—to get near a real dragon when given the choice. It was one thing to see a dragon landing in the distance from a viewing platform. It was quite another to have one grinning down at you from a mere foot away with teeth almost as long as you were tall.

Amber kissed her son's forehead. "See? Didn't I promise that you would get to see a dragon today?"

Raphek's grin widened and then slowly picked them both up in one large, black-taloned fist that was honestly disconcerting and carefully set them down onto the warm palm of his free—hand? Claw? She noted that it was indeed covered with a smaller type of red scales than the rest of his body.

"You aren't afraid of high places, are you?" Raphek asked.

"No…why?" Amber asked suspiciously.

She hoped to God that he didn't try to do any loop-de-loops like a freaking stunt plane. She might not be bothered by heights, but rollercoasters with loops on the other hand…

Besides, Matty was way too young to ride anything resembling a rollercoaster.

"You'll be traveling with me cupped protectively between my hands, the same as before," Raphek explained. "I'll try to keep my fingers loose enough that you'll both be able to see between them if you so choose. The view of our lands as well as our mountain from the air is a sight to see."

"Mommy! The dragon talks so loud!" Matty said in awe.

He swung his head to look up at Raphek. Amber couldn't help but smile at the way Matty's eyes lit up with such wonder. Maybe today's car chase and shootout hadn't damaged his psyche as much as she had feared if he could still smile in such delight only a few minutes later.

"I'll tell you a secret," she whispered as Raphek covered them with his other hand. "That nice man, Raphek, turns into the dragon."

"Cool!" Matty exclaimed.

There it was, his new favorite word. Amber hadn't realized how much she had needed to hear him say it in such a delighted tone after all the crap they had just gone through. Maybe it really was okay to let herself start to feel a little hopeful for the future.

CHAPTER FIVE

$\mathcal{N}$ow that Amber was in the frame of mind to truly experience soaring the skies with an actual dragon, even if riding encased within the hands of a dragon while peering at the rushing land-scape below through said dragon's fingers wasn't quite what fiction had imagined the experience would entail, it was still quite exhilarating. She didn't once feel queasy as both she and Matty peered between Raphek's red-scaled fingers.

They were just passing over a thriving city filled with unusually shaped white buildings that seemed more curves than straight edges. This was one city that Amber had never thought to lay eyes on, much less visit in her lifetime.

"Can we go down there, Mommy?" Matty asked as he squirmed in her lap, bursting with impatient energy.

Amber winced when Matty accidentally jostled her injured leg, making her throbbing wound flare up with a sharp pain, anew. "Maybe later, Matty. Right now, we're going to meet some of Raphek's friends."

"More dragons?" Matty asked without turning to look back at her.

"One of them, yes."

"Are there little dragons, too?" he asked excitedly.

She chuckled. "Probably." And wouldn't they be adorable, Amber couldn't help thinking.

North Point Mountain loomed behind the city, spectacular in its own right considering that they were in north Texas, a region that, until a few years ago, didn't have any mountains. She wondered what the dragons called it.

"We're almost there," Raphek's deep voice suddenly boomed all around them. "I'll be ascending again for a few beats and then landing on Sevek and Emma's balcony, so don't be alarmed."

Balcony? A helipad would be a more apt name for a surface big enough for a dragon to land comfortably.

The sun had started to set by the time they landed. When Raphek removed the hand that was cupped protectively over them, the light wasn't quite so blinding this time. Amber quickly took in her surroundings, surprised that the place they had landed did indeed look like a balcony, if a needlessly large one if the place hadn't been owned by dragons.

"Raphek!" a woman's voice abruptly exclaimed, followed by a series of guttural, incomprehensible words that didn't resemble any language Amber had ever heard.

A young woman with light brown hair, dressed in a pale blue, diaphanous gown, stepped out onto the balcony and froze like a deer in headlights when she caught sight of them sitting in Raphek's hand.

"Where did you…!" the woman trailed off as she stared at all of them with wide eyes.

"It's a long story," Raphek said with a sigh that nearly bowled Amber over, "but the short of it is this young human woman and her son were in need of immediate asylum within our lands. I happened to witness them being shot at by a group of human men along the border of our kingdom while out on patrol."

"Shot at?" the woman echoed in horror as she hurried over to them and fixed worried eyes first on Matty, then on Amber. Blue, *human*, eyes, Amber was quick to note. "Are you okay?"

"My son wasn't hurt," Amber assured her. "I was shot

in the leg, but Raphek slowed the bleeding with a makeshift bandage for me."

Now that the woman was closer, she looked a lot younger than Amber had first thought, early twenties, tops, but at the same time, Amber wouldn't have been surprised to learn that she was in her late teens.

"She needs a healer," Raphek added. "The bullet's still lodged into her calf muscle."

"There's no way that she can walk on that leg! Shift and carry them inside, Raphek," the woman commanded. She then turned to Amber and her features instantly softened. "I'm Emma by the way. I'm of the Rekkan House of Dancing Flames."

"Amber Davis," she said as Raphek carefully lowered them to the stone floor and then lumbered over to the opposite side of the balcony with a boatload more grace than something his size should possess to presumably shift into his human form, "and this is my son, Matthew. Matty for short."

Emma squatted down until she was eye-level with Matty, who was peering back at the brunette woman shyly. "Hi, Matty." She pointed at his dinosaur plushie. "Who's your friend?"

"T-rex," Matty replied bashfully.

"He's a cutie just like you," Emma said with a wink.

Matty smiled back at Emma tentatively. It was clear

that this woman knew how to handle young children. Was she a mother as well?

"Let's get you two inside," Raphek suddenly said beside her, making Amber jump.

She glanced up at him before she remembered that he was likely naked. However, this time Raphek was wearing a robe-like gold garment that tied closed at his side like a wide sash. Huh. Amber supposed it made sense for people who were constantly shifting to keep easy to throw on clothes out on their balconies. She was extremely grateful for small favors as the robe had saved her from what could have been the most awkward moment of her life given her current eye-level.

"May I?" Raphek asked as he knelt beside her and curled an arm around her back just short of touching.

Even so, Amber could feel his hotter-than-a-human's body heat through her blouse, and immediately wished she didn't as that same heat seemed to creep into her cheeks. As an adult, she had never been carried by anyone, and a dragon scooping her up with his claws didn't count. Although the same person had done both, the experience was like night and day when said dragon was now a gorgeous man that was only wearing a thin robe.

"Of—of course."

Raphek carefully scooped her up into a bridal carry,

Matty and all, and followed Emma through a pair of doors into a dim room with gray, stone walls and lit by what looked like several glass orbs of bright, pulsating white light spaced strategically along the walls. He set them down on a long, couch-like piece of furniture against a west-facing wall.

Matty slipped off her lap and burrowed into her side. He watched Emma sit down on Amber's other side with keen interest, still clutching his T-rex plushie tightly against his chest with one arm.

"I need to go report this to both the captain and to the king," Raphek told Emma. "My portion of the border remains unguarded."

"Go. We'll be fine here. Sevek will be home soon, but in the meantime, I'll make sure Amber and Matty are taken care of."

"I'll return the moment I'm able," Raphek promised. He turned to Amber. "His Majesty, King Dagon, will likely wish to speak with you sometime soon, but until then, rest and heal well until we meet again."

"We will, and thanks again for everything," Amber replied, still feeling a bit flustered.

The moment Raphek had closed the balcony doors behind him, she turned to Emma and said, "I'm so sorry for dumping my problems into your lap without even a heads up."

Emma waved her off as she stood. "Nonsense. I'm happy that Raphek thought to bring you to me first. Stretch your injured leg out on the couch, and I'll go call for a healer. Then I'll get you and your adorable son something cold to drink. Flying with dragons can give you an unbelievable case of cotton mouth. We'll talk some more then."

Really? Amber had just assumed that her mouth was so dry because of both shock and nerves.

"Thank you."

While they waited for Emma to return, Matty securely still burrowed into her side and eyes staring in the direction that Emma had left them, Amber's eyes roamed the room curiously. She tried to ignore the way her leg was starting to *really* throb and scream with an awful, burning pain, but mostly, she didn't want to think about the implications of what had happened to them at the energy shield. Not yet. She was more grateful than she could ever convey for this moment to just breathe that Raphek and Emma had gifted her. She knew better than to believe that everything would now be smooth sailing just because she and Matty had made it to her "sanctuary."

So far, except for the balcony, Emma's home resembled what Amber had pictured the rooms deep within a medieval stone castle might look like—high ceilings with wooden rafters, stone walls, and floors of the same stone. Various colorfully-patterned rugs that thankfully didn't look as though they had been made from animal pelts, possibly woven, covered the floor at the foot of all the oddly-shaped furniture meant for sitting as well as a large oval one in the room's center.

Then Amber's eyes fell on an awfully familiar looking tablet lying on a stone and stained-glass end table, and she gasped. There was no way that dragons from another world had developed something that looked identical to current human technology. The odds of that would be astronomical!

The last she had heard, the government had only allowed trade goods such as food and building materials to be offered to the dragons. No technology. So, how in the world had a *tablet* gotten here? Did Emma bring it here with her? That instantly made Amber wonder how *Emma* had ended up in Elysia South. Raphek had said she was the mate of one of his friends. Did "mate" mean she was a dragon's wife? Lover?

"I brought both ice water and tinik juice in case Matty doesn't care for the juice. It's a bit different than anything he's ever tasted, though the taste does remind me a little of fruit punch. Just a bit," Emma said cheerfully as she held out a wooden tray with several glossy, cream-colored mugs that looked to be ceramic and handmade.

Emma picked up one of the mugs and inspected its contents. "Thanks."

The liquid was thick like orange juice, but the color was more a bright mustard yellow. The smell coming from it was sweet but tinged with an aroma that put Amber in mind of the smell of rain. She took a cautious sip, and a sweet, fruity flavor exploded on her tongue in a combination unlike anything she had ever tasted, like a mixture of cherries and something like citrus but not quite really either. Amber doubted she would ever be able to explain it properly.

She offered the mug to Matty. "Want to try this cool-looking juice?"

"Does it taste like lemons?" Matty asked suspiciously, making a face.

Amber chuckled. "It *is* pretty yellow, but it's really sweet, I promise."

Matty bit his lip but then pulled the rim of the mug to his mouth. A little pink tongue abruptly dipped into the liquid before Amber could even react. His eyes widened. "It *is* good, Mommy!"

"Then that mug is all yours," Amber said with a laugh. "Sit back against the cushion and hold the mug with both hands. You don't want to get Emma's pretty couch dirty."

She accepted a second mug of juice from Emma. "I can't imagine what the fruit that made this looks like."

"It's round and smooth like a plum, the skin a bit darker yellow in color than the juice, and as big as a cantaloupe," Emma said as she sat the tray down on the end table next to the tablet. "The seeds are huge and also edible."

Seeing her opening, Amber nodded towards the end table as she took a bigger drink of the juice. "Is that tablet one of ours?"

Emma hesitated but then smiled. "Yeah. I brought it when I came here to live."

"How did you—"

"A long and tedious story that I'll tell you some other time if fate decides to give us that chance," Emma interjected. "Let's just get you and Matty taken care of first."

As if on cue, a sharp knock sounded somewhere to her left, saving Amber from having to reply as Emma excused herself and then hurried towards a thick, wooden door across the room. It was just as well since she had no idea what she would have said in response to such an obvious dodge and odd turn of phrase.

The woman that stepped across the threshold dressed in some type of cream and white tunic and robe combination straight out of a fantasy movie seriously didn't look human—like a supermodel on steroids once Amber was able to get a good look at her beneath the eerie, oscillating illumination of one of those strange light globes. She had straight, midnight-black hair that gleamed like strands of silk down to her mid-back and eyes the same unearthly shade of fire as Raphek's. She was also a good few inches taller than Emma, making Emma seem tiny in comparison.

This woman radiated *strength*, and Amber suddenly felt very intimidated in a way she hadn't with Raphek. Or maybe she had just been too much in shock earlier to notice. Could dragons emit a physical aura? They were shapeshifters after all, so wouldn't that involve some kind of—magic?

"Amber, this is Lady Serie of the House of Cinders," Emma introduced. "She's here to take care of your wound."

Oh. This was the healer Emma had called. Amber had just thought that "healer" was what the dragons called a doctor, but... Did dragon healers actually use *magic* to heal their patients rather than medicines and stitches? Was that why she'd had such a visceral reaction to the beautiful dragon-woman's presence alone? Was she sensing magic in her?

"Thank you so much—for coming here to see me so

quickly," Amber said, suddenly feeling as bashful as Matty, who was currently staring at their visitor with wide eyes.

Lady Serie's face melted into a soft smile, suddenly making her a thousand percent more approachable. "I am pleased to come," she replied, her words slightly more accented than Raphek's.

The healer gracefully knelt beside the couch down by Amber's legs and set down a large, cloth bag onto the rug Amber hadn't realized Lady Serie had been carrying. She opened it and began to pull out folded squares of white cloth that resembled linen and a couple of glass bottles with wax seals filled with a lime green and dark purple liquid of who-knew-what. Tinctures? Potions?

Amber had to bite her lip hard to keep from laughing aloud at the ridiculousness of her earlier thoughts about magic. *I must still be in shock to have let my imagination run so wild.*

"The flow of your blood throughout your body sounds weaker than I would like," Lady Serie said with a frown. She nodded towards the mug clutched in Amber's hands. "Drink all of that while I work. The tinik juice will help you replenish the blood you lost faster than time and rest."

"Would you like to watch some cartoons, Matty?"

Emma said as she sat down on the couch next to Matty and showed him her tablet.

"Go ahead," Amber said enthusiastically when he looked back at Emma with a hesitant look.

"Forrest Buddies?" he asked hopefully.

"Whatever you like," Emma promised, urging him to lean closer to her.

Amber was grateful to her hostess for the distraction. She really didn't want Matty to watch Lady Serie treat her gunshot wound, especially if it involved something like stitches or... Amber shuddered. Or *fire* for cauterization given they were fire dragons. Just how advanced was dragon medicine anyway?

Once Lady Serie had carefully removed Amber's denim bandage and turned her leg to a position that better exposed the bullet hole, the healer tutted. "Nasty things, guns. I have only seen them in videos, but it was enough to make me wish to never see them again. Give me a talon-to-fang battle in my scales rather than death that comes at you from a distance you cannot easily or quickly reach."

It was easy to forget that the woman tending her wound with such gentleness was also a fearsome, fire-breathing dragon with a wingspan the length of a football field and wicked looking claws that could probably cut her in half as easily as warm butter—until said woman said shocking things like that. Remembering the firmness of Raphek's scales, Amber wondered if a gun could even hurt a dragon.

Lady Serie carefully slipped one of the square cloths beneath her calf that was once again oozing blood. She then grabbed the bottle with the dark purple liquid and broke the seal.

"This will burn hot for only a couple of seconds," Lady Serie suddenly warned, "but then the pain will numb as though it had never been, not even an echo, I promise."

Before Amber could even process the healer's warning enough to feel alarmed, the dragon-woman poured the dark liquid over the bleeding bullet hole, and what felt like a hot poker abruptly jabbed into a wound that already burned with pain. Only years of keeping her screams of pain behind her teeth for fear of scaring and traumatizing Matty kept the scream of agony that rose in her throat from bursting forth as more than an aborted grunt.

One heartbeat, two, and then the pain inexplicably vanished, and Amber could breathe again without the threat of screaming.

"What—*was* that?" Amber asked, sounding winded.

"A medicine to stop the bleeding that also has anesthetic properties," Lady Serie answered as she poured some of the lime green liquid onto a clean cloth. "I will use this one to—sterilize, I believe is the term your people use. Only then can I safely remove the bullet."

Amber silently watched the healer work with the cutesy voices of a cartoon as a strange backdrop. It was a bit disconcerting that she couldn't feel even a hint of pressure as Lady Serie used a long and thin tool that resembled a giant metal toothpick and another metal tool with a flat plate at the end like a miniature yard hoe to begin digging out the bullet. It was as though she were poking at someone else's leg.

She glanced over at Matty and Emma worriedly. Someone digging into her leg was definitely something she didn't want her three-year-old son to see. Thankfully, Matty was completely engrossed with his cartoon and didn't show any signs of having witnessed any of the horror show happening with her leg.

Amber turned back to her crude surgery in enough time to see Lady Serie pop out the bloody bullet. She wrapped it up in a used cloth and then spent a few seconds cleaning up the bit of blood extracting the bullet had left behind on the skin around the wound with more of the green disinfectant.

"Now, don't be alarmed," Lady Serie said, her lips suddenly stretching into that same soft smile she had w orn earlier. "I know this isn't something Terrans have ever seen, but my *Lockran* won't hurt you, either."

Lockran?

Then Amber forgot to breathe when Lady Serie's hands began to glow a pale blue as she placed them over Amber's wound. While Amber felt absolutely nothing on her numbed leg, all the hair on her arms and the nape of her neck rose as the air around her suddenly seemed electrically charged.

It could have been ten minutes or an hour she watched the dragon-woman's glowing hands, before Lady Serie moved them away from her leg and the blue glow faded completely. Where a bullet hole once lay was now a slightly raised pucker of pink skin, now looking weeks instead of an hour or so old.

"Magic..." Amber whispered in awe.

"Yeah, magic," Emma said with a chuckle. "Welcome to the world of dragons."

CHAPTER SIX

Despite his hands having been naturally cleansed as usual between form shifts, Raphek could still feel Amber's warm blood staining his human hands as he knelt before his king, and the ghost sensation made him itch to bare his teeth and roar in fury.

Just seeing the Terran woman with the golden hair curled protectively around the sobbing little boy with desperation twisting her face even as her own bleeding injury went ignored had instantly ignited the Fire deep within him. After snatching Amber and Matty through the shield to safety, Raphek had barely stopped himself from sticking his snout through the shield as well in order to roar his ignited Fire upon the men who had dared shoot their foul weapons at a mother and her child. Thank the Sacred Fires that the child had not been shot as well, or he likely *wouldn't* have been able to stop himself. No matter the reason, burning humans to ash would have been a PR nightmare for the Rekkan.

Of course, bringing a couple of Terrans into Elysia South in full view of other Terrans when such an action was forbidden by the US government had a high probability of causing its own complications that could become just as bad of a PR nightmare if they weren't careful. While he would never regret saving those who were helpless, Raphek hated that the king would likely bear the larger brunt of the consequences of his actions.

His Majesty *hated* dealing with the powers that be in Washington.

"Not that I think you should have ignored such brutality happening right under your nose, but..." King Dagon trailed off with a heavy sigh as he leaned back against the end of the long conference table.

"I know," Raphek acknowledged grimly.

"And right next to one of those blasted viewing platforms," the king continued. "I knew agreeing to such daily observation would, as my brother would say, come back to bite us in the ass. Frankly, I'm just surprised something like this didn't happen sooner. You're sure that the woman's wound wasn't life-threatening?"

"The wound was small, and didn't hit anything vital,"

Raphek assured him. "I'm sure the healer Emma called for her has finished treating her by now."

"Asylum," Dagon said thoughtfully. "Her situation must be dire indeed to plead help from a kingdom still relatively new to her own world and not from her people's own authorities."

"Amber said that she believed Elysia South was the one place on this earth that her son would be safe from his father, who comes from a powerful family. I still don't know the details, but apparently, the bastard not only threatened to kill her if she tried to leave him but also recently hurt the boy."

The king's eyes narrowed. "A very real threat considering what occurred at the shield. To deliberately hurt something as precious as a child... The rotten depths some beings will fall to truly astounds me sometimes."

For the second time, Raphek nearly bared his teeth and growled at the memory of Matty's frightened sobs as his mother lay bleeding on the ground begging for help. However, no matter how angry the memory made him, the king was definitely not the audience for it.

"Captain Cabris has assigned another to my patrol for the remainder of the day," he said, a hint of growl still in his tone.

Dammit. He was before the king! He really needed to

settle down. Didn't Airon always quip that he was the only levelheaded one of their closest friends?

Yet, I think no Draknos could be calm after witnessing a child in danger...

"I thought it best I start determining whether or not the human media has started reporting on the incident rather than return to my patrol," Raphek continued, his tone much steadier this time, to his relief. "I don't regret saving them, but I do regret that it may have come at the cost of inadvertently allowing the Terran military to learn a bit about the nature of our shields."

"Indeed. I imagine seeing you breech it so easily without affecting the integrity of the whole even the slightest will raise a few eyebrows in Washington," Dagon said dryly, "but what's done is done. For the time being, I will grant our unexpected guests temporary asylum as they are both obviously in mortal danger while on Terran soil, but Amber Davis will need to make a formal request for asylum, to plead her case, before me and another witness of the Court, tomorrow at the latest.

"Raphek, you will be their advocate in all things from this moment forward. I think it best to suspend your patrol duties for the next few days to both attend to the young family's basic needs as well as to monitor the ramifications of what occurred at the shield through the Terrans' media."

Raphek bowed his head. "That was my intention. I rather unceremoniously showed up with them on Emma and Sevek's balcony. I don't wish to inconvenience them any more than I already have, so Amber and Matthew will of course stay with me in my home for as long as you decree."

The king waved his hand dismissively. "I doubt Emma sees it that way. That our new guests are of her people will undoubtably see her at your door between her own duties wishing to help anyway she can. Briana, too, for that matter... Perhaps my brother's mate would be a better interrogator than I for Amber's petition—and in a more casual setting than this council room."

He paused, his eyes going distant for a long moment. He then gestured for Raphek to rise.

"Bring Amber and Matthew to my personal residence for the midday meal tomorrow. After such a trying experience today, it's best to make them feel as secure as possible if we hope to receive all the answers we need, because Raphek, though it pains me to say it, we *cannot* afford to allow this terrible affair to undermine all the goodwill we have managed to build up with the Terrans."

"Understood, Your Majesty."

EMMA ANSWERED the door mere seconds after he knocked. Raphek was immediately on high alert. Was something wrong?

His friend brought a finger to her lips in the Terran gesture for silence before he could open his mouth to speak. He nodded, and she ushered him inside. Emma then pointed at a section of her seating, and the tension instantly drained out of his body.

Both Amber and Matty were cuddled up together asleep, stretched out on the large cushions.

"Balcony," Emma whispered.

Once they were outside with the doors firmly closed, Raphek spoke for the first time, "The healing went well?"

Emma grinned. "Yes. Amber was sufficiently awed by Lady Serie's methods."

"Understandable given that the Terrans—present company excluded—have no idea we can perform magic. They still believe that our shield is something technological rather than magical."

"Well, a few Terrans a lot smarter than me have posited that the technology of advanced civilizations would likely be indistinguishable from what we would think of now as magic, so I don't think it would really matter in the long run if Terrans did find out some of the Draknos wield magic," Emma replied cheekily.

Raphek frowned. Would they really? Although it was obvious Emma was just teasing him, the thought that the Terran leaders might see technology and magic so interchangeably might be cause for alarm—but no. He couldn't worry about that right now. He had far more pressing problems on his plate to go reaching for another serving while his plate was teetering precariously on the edge of the table.

"An argument for another time, I think," he said with a sigh. "The child? How is he faring given everything he's had to endure today? His mother injured right before his eyes, being so near a dragon, and then having to stay in a place that is likely very alien to what he's accustomed to."

Emma's amused expression abruptly turned deathly serious. "Honestly? I think Matty's adjusted to everything a little too well for a little boy that's practically still a baby. It's as though seeing his mother hurt isn't new at all. After the healing, Amber understandably needed to sleep. I was worried that she wouldn't because she didn't want to leave Matty awake and alone with a virtual stranger.

"However, it's as though Matty could sense how exhausted Amber was, and it was *him* that suggested that it was naptime and 'would Mommy take a nap with me.' That little boy has seen some things, I think. Some very bad things, and I'm not talking about being shot at today."

Raphek once again felt the need to growl, but he suppressed it—barely. The fact that it was becoming harder to keep his anger behind his teeth about the whole rotten incident was troubling.

"I don't know the details, but yes, they both have endured violence in their pasts at the hands of Matty's father."

Emma's eyes narrowed angrily. "An abuser?"

"I believe Amber's exact word for him was a 'monster.' It's no coincidence that they were at that viewing platform today. Amber came seeking asylum from us."

"And what does the king say about that?" Emma asked with a raised eyebrow.

"He's granted it—at least temporarily until Amber can plead her case formally. Given the potential political ramifications of the situation, His Majesty, of course, wishes to speak with her as soon as possible. Carefully. Thus, he's invited them to an informal midday meal with just him, Princess Briana, and me. As a royal, the princess can serve as a witness for Amber's petition for asylum as well as a secondary questioner."

Emma nodded. "No one is better at making someone feel at ease than the princess."

"In the meantime, His Majesty has agreed that they should remain under my care for the time being." Raphek glanced over at the double doors and frowned. "I had planned to move them to my home right away, but after your words, I'm loathed to wake them…"

"They, as well as you, are more than welcome to stay here for the night," Emma said instantly.

Raphek hesitated for a few more seconds before he relented. Amber and Matty's comfort was more important than his usual dislike of imposing on his friends' kindness.

"Then—I'll need to borrow your tablet. I need to determine just how much my actions today have shaken the status quo between our two peoples."

"Of course. Anything you need." Emma pressed her hand against her chest. "We can help you with that, as well. I feel Sevek heading this way, and there's nothing more he likes to do after eating than to scroll through all the Terran news sites on the tablet for a couple of hours, especially now that Lily sent him a larger one than mine a couple of weeks ago when Airon came to report. He was like a kid on Christmas morning."

Some of the tension in Raphek's shoulders eased. "Thank you, my friend."

CHAPTER SEVEN

*A*mber wasn't sure what had awakened her, but the moment she moved her body and realized that Matty was no longer snuggled up against her, she was instantly wide awake. She bolted upright, her heart pounding a million-miles-a-second as she frantically scanned an oddly illuminated room that still hadn't quite blurred into vision. "Matty!"

"It's all right, Amber," a vaguely familiar male voice said placatingly from her right.

Amber's head turned to the voice so sharply that her neck popped loudly, her hands instinctually shooting up as though to ward off an attacker. The dragon-shifter, Raphek, sat on the end of the long couch she and Matty had been sleeping on, his orange-tinted eyes full of wary concern.

Amber drew in a shaky breath and slowly lowered her arms as she tried to clear the last foggy remnants of sleep from her mind. *It wasn't a dream...Matty and I really were saved by a dragon! Wait...!*

"Where's—"

Raphek pointed across the room and her eyes anxiously followed. "Your son is there with Emma on that rug playing with Emma and Sevek's pet mog."

Mog?

The first thought Amber had when she saw said creature that currently had its back to her and was being pet within an inch of its life by her son was, *They have a sheep as a pet?*

Then she did a doubletake. Yeah...last time she checked, sheep didn't have large white paws like a dog or long, floppy ears like a bunny...

"Mommy! Come pet Jaws, too!" Matty said excitedly.

The fluffy creature—mog—stood so docilly while Matty loved on it that Amber almost believed that it was just a rather large plushie. Why in the world would Emma name it Jaws? Did it like to chew things? Or did the word "jaws" mean something else in the Draknar language?

Emma chuckled. "From the look on your face, you're probably wondering why I named such a marsh-mallow after a shark. Don't be alarmed, but once you see his teeth, you'll understand. He doesn't bite, I promise."

Amber surged to her feet in alarm anyway before she remembered the gunshot wound on her leg. A split-second later, Raphek was at her side gently grasping her shoulders with hands as hot as a heating pad as she wobbled and nearly crumpled to the ground, not from any kind of pain, but an intense spell of sudden dizziness.

"Easy," he chided, his low voice inexplicably sending shivers up her spine. "While your wound is mostly healed, your body, rather than Lady Serie's magic, did most of the work. You'll probably feel weak for another day or so."

Her mind whirling in a million different directions, Amber allowed Raphek to coax her to sit back down onto the couch. "Thanks," she said hoarsely. She then refocused on Matty, who was now looking at her with wide, confused eyes. "Mommy's just a bit dizzy right now, sweetie. I'll come pet Jaws with you in a minute."

"Your cheeks are much too pale," Raphek said, the scrutiny of his eyes making her squirm. She was *not* used to being fussed over—not since she had gotten married, anyway, and definitely not by men too gorgeous to be real. "Let me go get you some juice."

Only when he released her shoulders and stepped off

to the side did Amber realize that there was an unfamiliar dark-haired man seated on another long couch across the room. He had what looked like a tablet clutched in both hands, but his gaze was fixed keenly on her.

"Oh! I'm sorry, I-I didn't see you there—" Amber stammered as her entire body instinctually tensed.

A dragon guard waiting to interrogate her? The black, tunic-like outfit he wore was different than the guard uniforms she had seen the dragon-shifters wear on TV years ago during the Dragon Summit. A quick glance at the windows facing the balcony showed only darkness. Just how long had she been sleeping?

The unknown man's intense expression melted into a friendly smile as he set his tablet down onto his lap. "I'm Emma's mate, Sevek. It's nice to meet you, Amber Davis."

Amber relaxed minutely, though she still rung her hands anxiously in her lap. "Oh, of course. It's nice to meet you, too, though I'm really sorry for troubling you and Emma with my mess."

Emma sighed heavily. "As if watching over your little cutie is any kind of trouble," she interjected before Sevek could reply.

"But—I slept too long, and now it's the middle of the night! I don't want to keep you from your sleep any more than I already have!" she protested. "You all probably have work tomorrow, and—"

"It's no trouble, really," Raphek cut in earnestly as he handed her a mug of the same yellow juice she had drunk earlier. "Draknos have no need to sleep."

"At all?" Amber asked incredulously, looking from him to Sevek to Emma and back.

"Completely unfair, isn't it?" Emma said with an annoyed huff, but she was smiling.

Amber couldn't even imagine it. "It sounds exhausting, actually."

"I suppose it can be at times," Raphek mused.

"Can't miss what you've never experienced," Sevek added with a shrug.

A strange, high-pitched sound had Amber looking over at the three on the rug again. Matty had gotten up and was on his way over to her. The mog was in the process of turning around to likely follow him. Then Amber nearly choked on her mouthful of tinik juice when she finally got her first look at Jaws's face.

While the mog's facial proportions and snout were rather sheep-like, that's really where the comparison ended. Its eyes were about twice the size of a sheep's, oval-shaped, and a startling cobalt blue that seemed to glow with a type of bioluminescence rather than the result of something like night shine. However, what had

Amber really gaping in shock was the seemingly dozens of sharp, pointed teeth stretched across a wide mouth as though grinning at her. *Grinning* at her!

Jaws let out that strange high-pitched sound she had heard earlier as Matty climbed onto her lap, nearly making her slosh her juice all over both of them, she was so focused on the mog. Before Amber could react, the mog rose onto its hind legs and put its two front paws heavily onto her left thigh. He then looked up at her with the roundest, most pleading eyes she had ever seen on an animal juxtaposed with a grin that was a mockery of everything holy.

"Jaws!" Emma scolded as she climbed to her feet. "He is such an attention-whore, I swear. I'm sorry, but he's used to being around a lot of kids who spoil him rotten with cuddles and pets."

Matty took the mug from Amber's hands. "Pet him, Mommy!"

"You have kids?" Amber asked as she carefully ran a hand over Jaws's head, still unable to take her eyes off those nightmarish teeth. The mog closed his eyes and made a low sound like a hum that she could more feel than hear.

"No, no. I teach all the little dragons English as well as all things Terran to both children and adults," Emma said. "They love it when I bring Jaws to the classroom."

"Oh, you're a teacher," Amber said. "So, the government sent you here? As something like a cultural ambassador?"

When Emma didn't answer right away, Amber finally tore her eyes away from Jaws's teeth to look up at her hostess. She couldn't quite decipher the other woman's expression, but one thing was clear. She had inadvertently stepped into a minefield.

"No, never mind," Amber said hastily. "That was awfully nosy of me to ask, wasn't it?"

Emma shook her head. "It's fine. My situation is a bit complicated, and I'm not used to answering questions about it. I—think it's best that we just leave it at that, for both our sakes."

"…and not mention meeting Emma at all to any other Terrans," Sevek added, his tone deathly serious.

Yes, definitely a minefield.

"I won't. You have my word," Amber told him just as seriously.

"Mommy? I'm hungry," Matty abruptly announced, and just like that, the thick tension in the room dissipated.

"I wasn't sure if he had any food allergies, so I didn't give him anything other than juice when he woke up," Emma said apologetically.

"He doesn't," Amber replied. "Well, at least with earth food."

"Don't worry," Emma said. "If you'd rather, I can make you two something Terran tonight. It's probably best to keep things familiar anyway given all the turmoil Matty's experienced today. You both will have plenty of opportunity to taste Elysian cuisine tomorrow when you and Raphek dine with the king and Princess Briana for lunch."

"The king has agreed to hear your petition for asylum," Raphek explained as her eyes widened in sudden shock. "He thought you would be more comfortable in a more casual setting than having to speak before the entire Court at the foot of his throne."

"*King Dagon...wants me to...*" Amber trailed off, her stomach dropping into her feet like a lead boulder.

She never in a million years had expected to talk to the firedrake king at all! Had Garrett's father already started enough of a shitstorm that the *king* felt the need to deal with her directly?

"Don't be nervous," Emma said. "The royals are some of the kindest people you'll ever meet, but Amber, let me be frank. You must know that what Raphek did to protect you and Matty at the border—in full view of Terran witnesses, no less—has put the kingdom in a bit of a precarious spot."

"Yes," Amber agreed quietly, her eyes lowering as a fresh wave of guilt washed through her.

A warm finger lifted her chin until she reluctantly met Raphek's uncanny, yet beautiful, eyes. "And I would do it again, regardless, and without regret," he said firmly. "Not one soul in this kingdom would ever condemn you for trying to protect your son. Never doubt that. Nor will they condemn me for it."

"No one would come here, of all places, to beg for asylum without a damn good reason," Emma said. "Just be sure to leave nothing out tomorrow when you talk to the king. Secrets, no matter how well intentioned, tend to come back to bite everyone in the ass." She grimaced. "Believe me, I know."

Unfortunately, in Amber's case, it was an omission rather than a secret that had the potential to make her entire world come crashing down. It was something she had planned to never reveal if she had managed to safely enter Elysia South under the protections of sanctuary with none being the wiser. Yet somehow, Garrett, that utter bastard, had known she was planning to run with Matty and had planned accordingly to thwart her at the worst possible moment.

And now, because of that monster, she would likely have to run again to avoid causing more problems to a kingdom filled with wonderous and kind people that never asked to be dragged into her nightmare of a life. But maybe, just maybe, if she played her cards right, Matty wouldn't have to run with her. It wouldn't matter if Garrett tried to finish the job Raphek had interrupted.

As long as Matty was forever beyond Garrett's clutches, then Amber would gladly consider her life to be a worthy trade.

CHAPTER EIGHT

For what felt like the billionth time in the last five minutes, Amber tugged nervously at the thin skirt of the tunic-dress hybrid that Emma had given her to wear for her lunch with the king and princess as she followed Raphek to what Emma had called the "lifts." She was so nervous about what amounted to an interrogation no matter how much her new dragon acquaintances insisted otherwise that even the crazy description of the Elysian version of an elevator couldn't distract her.

Although Amber had wanted to meet the royals dressed in what she felt was something a ton more appropriate than the torn and dirty jeans she had arrived in, she had thought it best that Matty be dressed in his own clothes rather than have Emma either buy him a new outfit or borrow one. She already felt guilty enough taking advantage of their hospitality as it was and damn sure didn't want to drag yet another unwitting Draknos family into her problems.

Luckily, Matty viewed their trek to the royals' home as a grand adventure. He constantly tugged at their joined hands excitedly as he pointed out things that caught his attention while they walked down the gray, rock-faced corridors with their dragon...host? Sponsor? Minder? Amber wasn't altogether sure.

The dragon-shifter had certainly made sure that she and Matty were taken care of from the moment they had entered Elysia South, but was that attentiveness out of true altruism or something else? She hadn't quite known how to ask without coming across as ungrateful or worse, suspicious, so she said nothing at all rather than risk accidentally damaging her case for asylum. As a result, that uncertainty had sat in the back of her mind all morning like a growing cancer, a dangerous addition to her already growing anxiety about her upcoming lunch date with the royals.

Allowing herself to be lured into a false sense of security at this point was beyond stupid, but within Emma and Sevek's home, she had been doing exactly that, taking people at face value when she *knew* how dangerous that was. Consequently, she was now tied into knots over self-inflicted uncertainties concerning the dragon-man walking beside her when she could least afford that kind of distraction.

Raphek was a part of the Royal Guard, after all, as the black and red uniform he currently wore blatantly reminded her. He had saved them, yes, but he certainly owed them nothing more. That he was still with her playing guide was probably because he had been assigned to keep an eye on them by his superiors until the king could decide what to do with them—and wasn't that thought scary. A monarch's word was considered absolute law in a true monarchy, wasn't it? If so, then why the hell was she wasting time fretting about Raphek and his friends' motives rather than the man who now held Matty's future in his hands?

If King Dagon decided that granting them permanent asylum would be too politically damaging for his kingdom—she and Matty *had* broken US law by entering Elysia South—she had no doubt that Raphek would plop them back across the energy shield if ordered...

Way to throw everyone under the bus before King Dagon can even ask his first question, Amber thought in sudden disgust. *God—not every act of kindness has to have an ulterior motive! Not everyone is like* him*!*

"Raphek!"

Amber started out of her self-deprecating thoughts as a young, chestnut-haired woman dressed in a red and black garment similar in cut to her own outfit hurried towards them.

"I'm so glad I caught you before you made it to the lifts," she said in a startlingly familiar Texas twang.

Puzzled, Amber took a closer look at the dragon-woman's face and with a jolt, realized that she wasn't a dragon-woman at all. She had seen this woman's face plastered all over social media ever since the Dragon Summit. She was Briana Wright, the human woman from Texas who had married a dragon prince!

"Has something happened, Your Highness?" Raphek asked, confirming the woman's identity.

Princess Briana nodded. "Unfortunately, and sooner than any of us expected." She then turned to Amber and held out her hand, "I'm sorry to meet you like this out in the hallway, but I'm Princess Briana of the House of the Red Flame. It's nice to meet you, Amber."

Amber accepted the princess's firm handshake. "It's nice to meet you, too."

The House of the Red Flame... But wasn't that Raphek's...

Amber turned her head sharply to Raphek and blurted, "You're a *royal*?"

"Not in the way I think you mean," Raphek replied slowly. "I am untitled."

"But what—"

"I think this is a conversation better had somewhere more private," Princess Briana interjected. "I think your home would be best, Raphek. The king will likely be tied up for a good while, so I, alone, will hear Amber's petition for asylum. You'll serve as her witness in my stead."

Raphek bowed his head solemnly. "Of course."

As if Amber weren't nervous enough already, she could practically taste the tension rolling off her two escorts as Amber led Matty after them out of the corridor into a vast space. At least a dozen or so people were either heading for or stepping off the large, recessed circles in the stone floors that Emma had explained were the physical components of the mountain's lifts.

While the princess nodded at all those who passed their group in greeting, no one tried to speak to either her or Raphek. They did, however, stare at Matty and her, a couple with openly curious expressions. Even from afar, their blonde hair would have given away that they weren't Draknos. As far as she had ever seen, the firedrakes were all dark-haired. It was a bit disconcerting to realize that both she and Matty would so easily be identified anywhere and from any distance within Elysia South just because of their hair color.

"My home is located on the level just below the king's," Raphek said as they stepped onto one of the outermost recessed circles that was a few feet separated from the others and guarded by four men wearing the same uniform as Raphek.

The guards, too, had eyed Amber and Matty with curiosity. That no one so far had showed even a hint of hostility towards Terrans in their midst made Amber's anxiety ease a fraction.

Amber picked up Matty and held him against her chest. "Remember, sweetie," she warned, "these elevators are different than the ones you're used to. Even though you won't be able to move your arms and legs until we get to the top, you can still blink your eyes and talk. Just keep your eyes on me."

"Okay," Matty said, opting to lay his head against her chest as he did whenever he was being bashful.

"Probably a good idea for his first ride," Princess Briana said with a fond smile.

Even though she knew what to expect, Amber still felt a moment of claustrophobia once Raphek activated the lift spell with a few Draknar words, and she felt the magic entrap her. Matty let out a short gasp, but that was his only reaction as the stone disc began to slowly rise.

"Still okay, sweetie?" Amber asked once they had reached their destination and the spell had released them.

"I feel itchy," he complained.

Amber rubbed at his back and arms briskly. "Better?"

"Yeah." He raised his head a little and looked around. "We're still inside the rocks!"

Amber chuckled. "Yes, we just went higher. We're going to Raphek's house now."

Matty turned to Raphek. "Do you have a mog, too?"

"No, little one. I'm sorry."

Amber was a bit surprised to see that the layout of Raphek's place was pretty much identical to Emma and Sevek's, down to the furniture, placement of the rugs, and globes of lights scattered around the room. Only the colors of the fabrics were different, chocolate browns with accents of reds in the rugs to Emma's cremes and pastel blues.

"Don't worry about the midday meal, Raphek," Princess Briana said as they all sat down on one of his couches. "The king's staff will be bringing food here shortly."

"Do you have yellow juice like Emma?" Matty asked the princess hopefully.

She smiled. "You can have whatever kind of juice you want. I'm Briana. What's your name, cutie?"

"Matthew Johnson," Matty replied with a grin.

Amber nearly swallowed her tongue. Shit!

"Johnson, huh?" the princess said, though she looked at Amber, not Matty, as she spoke.

There was no surprise in those green eyes. She *knew.*

"Yes, Johnson," Amber confirmed, her shoulders slumping.

She paused. Well, no use hiding it now.

"Davis is my maiden name." She was relieved that her tone of steady and not the least bit defensive.

Princess Briana nodded. "Thank you for your honesty."

Raphek looked from the princess to Amber, frowning. "What am I missing?"

"Dagon said that you were monitoring the Terrans' social media after your meeting with him yesterday," Princess Briana said.

He nodded. "Sevek and I spent all night and morning combing through the internet looking for either videos or just mentions of the incident at the viewing platform, but we both found nothing."

"The king is currently on a video chat with President Mitchell. Apparently, a few senators are currently raising a fuss about complaints of dragons stealing people from the viewing platforms."

Amber's blood ran cold.

"Leading the charge is a senator from Texas. Henry Johnson."

"Where there's people, there's usually at least one person capturing video," Raphek grumbled. "Did the senator show the president a video of me bringing Amber and Matty through the energy shield?"

"No, and that's what worries me. The president told Dagon that the FBI have launched an investigation into the complaints. She gave him no details—no names of the missing, no specific evidence. Dagon, of course, has promised the president to do the same."

It felt as though an invisible hand was squeezing her neck tightly. "You're right to worry," Amber said thickly. "He one hundred percent already has the 'proof.' He's already controlling the narrative. It may not seem like it, but this is that bastard's way of sending a message to me, and me alone." Amber had to force the next sentence out. "He's already won."

Princess Briana's eyes narrowed. "How so?"

"If the king denies that Raphek reached across the barrier and brought Matty and me into Elysia South, then the senator won't bother sending the video to the FBI. He has too much of a personal stake in the matter.

It would look suspicious. He'll just anonymously upload an edited version of the video to the internet and let social media do what it does best. It will, of course, leave out his hired thugs running me off the road and then shooting at us. Or me begging Raphek for help. It'll just look exactly like the complaint the president has already raised with King Dagon."

"If that happens, then we can kiss years of goodwill between the Rekkan and the Terrans goodbye," Briana said flatly.

Only the thought of Matty seeing her fall apart kept the tears of despair at bay. Amber, of course, had a plan for this particular kind of worst-case scenario, one she had desperately prayed would never see the light of day.

"Don't worry," Amber said. "I *won't* let that happen. I'll—leave the kingdom as soon as we finish here."

"To be murdered? I don't think so," Raphek growled, his tone so menacing that it sent a literal shiver down Amber's spine.

She was even more taken aback by his eyes that seemed to glow with red flames. It was both beautiful and a bit frightening. More dragon magic?

"He's right," Princess Briana seconded firmly. "You told Raphek that your husband has hurt Matty. I would also be willing to bet my title that you asked Emma to borrow something with long sleeves for today's meeting to hide the fact that you have bruises on your arms that are older than the violence done to you yesterday. A man who would so callously destroy the lives of thousands of innocent people by spreading lies just to placate his monster of a son should *not* be rewarded for such a despicable abuse of power."

Amber twitched. She did indeed have several bruises on her arms, impressions of Garrett's fingers where he had violently and cruelly grabbed her with the intent to cause pain during bouts of his usual temper over the past month. Although she knew it was seriously messed up for her to feel it, shame burned her cheeks.

"No, he shouldn't," Amber said quietly, "but—if Matty can stay here, if King Dagon will at least grant *him* permanent asylum, then that's more than enough for me. The king can tell the president the true story and that we both left after my injuries were treated. I'll head north as though I'm still trying to run with Matty and do my best to disappear." *Live on the streets if I have to...*

Given that her car, money, and all her documents of identity where now likely in the senator's hands, that would probably happen.

The princess sighed. "You really must have a low opinion of people if you think we would let you do any of that just to save our own skins."

"But...!"

"If there's anything my brother-in-law hates, it's corrupt assholes like the senator trying to force his hand," Princess Briana said. "A child in harm's way? Even more so. I will consider this meeting your official petition for asylum. You and Matty will, of course, be welcome to stay in the kingdom while the king decides the most appropriate way forward that is best for *everyone*. Raphek has already been granted leave by the king to host you in his home as your patron for as long as you both need."

Amber turned to Raphek sharply. "Oh! But, but I—I couldn't possibly inconvenience you any more than we already—"

"If I thought hosting you were any sort of inconvenience, I would not have offered to do it," Raphek replied bluntly, his expression serious and unblinking.

"The Draknos are not like Terrans," Princess Briana said, her expression so kind and motherly despite her apparent youth that it made Amber's eyes suddenly tighten with the threat of tears. "They have bottomless wells of patience that can seem quite unfathomable to a society that seems to have next to none."

Raphek snorted. "Hardly bottomless. You Terrans just can't sit still."

A sudden knock at the door had Amber stiffening and Raphek jumping to his feet.

"Food is here," he announced, offering Amber a boyish smile that made her cheeks heat up in reaction as he headed for the door.

"All Draknos have noses better than a bloodhound," Princess Briana said, shaking her head with a small smile of amusement. "Remember that."

Amber stared at his retreating back without comment, discomfited at her reaction to him, and then looked over at Matty sitting quietly beside her, his eyes on Raphek, too. She wondered what he was thinking. She hoped to God that his emotions weren't as tumultuous as hers were at the moment.

"Is it really okay for us to stay here, Your Highness?" she couldn't help asking again.

"Please, there's no need to address me so formally outside of Court or whenever I'm being official," the princess said as they both watched a handful of men and women carry in several covered dishes of food in what looked like containers made of a reddish clay. "Just 'Briana' is fine, and yes, it's really okay. Raphek's a pretty serious, unassuming soul. You couldn't ask for a better patron to help you get back on your feet, whether that turns out to be here within Elysia South or somewhere else in the world. For now, all you need to worry about is trying a few of our Elysian dishes, taking care of your son, and healing. You let Dagon and I worry about Henry Johnson."

Amber's heart once again clenched painfully with guilt. "You shouldn't have to," she said miserably.

Briana placed a comforting hand onto her shoulder. "And neither should you. Now, come. Let's get this little man fed, and while we eat, you can give us a little bit more of your backstory, as much as you feel comfortable sharing. We need as much ammunition against Senator Johnson and his son as you can give us. Plus, I'm sure you have a million questions about life in our cities."

"At least," Amber agreed, offering the other woman a shaky smile.

Especially about her new patron, because unlike the princess, she wasn't so sure it was a good idea to live completely at the mercy of another man, no matter how kind and "unassuming" he seemed at the moment.

After all, she had been fooled once before by a charming smile and good looks.

CHAPTER NINE

$\mathcal{A}$mber hadn't realized exactly how nervous she was to be left alone with Raphek until the moment the door closed behind Briana and silence hung heavily in the air.

She didn't even have Matty as a natural buffer between them as he had fallen asleep on the couch about thirty minutes prior. No TV or even a radio, either. No more tasks for her to do other than "rest" even though her leg hadn't hurt once since it had been healed, and she wasn't even the least bit tired. In fact, she was so keyed up that she was nearly ready to jump clean out of her skin with anxiety.

Raphek was right about Terrans. She had never been very good at sitting still.

What the hell was she supposed to do now?

In all her plans to get Matty safely into Elysia South, Amber hadn't thought much about what they would do past that seemingly impossible accomplishment beyond vague notions of her finding any kind of work she could and learning more about the Draknos culture.

Maybe asking to join Emma in her classes was the answer? Matty would, at the very least, have other children to play with. He was nearly four. Was it possible to enroll Matty in some type of school at that age?

"If you wish to sleep a bit somewhere less narrow than my couch, you and Matty can use my meditation room," Raphek offered abruptly, drawing her gaze back to the handsome face she had been studiously trying not to look at sitting in an overstuffed chair adjacent to the couch that resembled a large, cloth-covered beanbag.

"Oh, well, thanks but I'm—I'm fine. I was just thinking about—things," she finished lamely.

"Thoughts can be especially exhausting," he said sympathetically. "If you like, I can continue telling you a bit about our cities and culture while Matty continues to nap. Then when he wakes, how about I take you both down to the city beyond this mountain for a short tour? We can also take the opportunity to find you something suitable for bedding as well as clothing."

"I would love that," she replied sincerely, something like excitement igniting within her. Then reality came and dropped a truth bomb onto her head. "But—Matty and I literally have nothing more than the clothes we came in. I had brought a backpack full of some minor food supplies, a couple of changes of clothes, identification, and of course, money, but I was in such a hurry to get Matty out of the car after those bastards ran me off the road that it got left behind. Only Matty's T-rex plushie made it across."

"Your Terran money would have been useless here, anyway," Raphek said. "Jewels are our currency here."

Amber perked up. "Jewels as in diamonds and rubies?" She pulled off her diamond wedding ring and held it up to him. "Could I use the diamond from this?"

Raphek reached over and took the ring from her. He spent a moment scrutinizing it. "I've never seen this type of earth jewel outside of a video or photo. It much resembles an Elysian jewel known as a Mitnokt that is often used as a focus by the Mikkan in their higher level spellcraft, but I can tell just from its absence of any discernible smell that it's a completely different jewel. From what Emma has told me, diamonds are one of the hardest natural substances in your world."

"Yeah, we use them for cutting and polishing stuff as well as for jewelry," Amber said. "So, it's worthless here?"

"No item from your world is worthless," he said.

"Something like this would trade well within several different markets, I think." He handed it back to her. "You just can't use it as currency."

Amber sighed in disappointment. "Then how am I going to buy—"

"You and Matty are guests of our kingdom. Until that status changes, then all your needs will be taken care of courtesy of the royal coffers."

Amber stared back at Raphek in shock. "But..." Her voice trailed off, unsure of what to say.

Before she could react, Raphek stood and reached down to clasp one of her hands between the furnace of his own. The warmth against the clamminess of her own hands made her shiver.

"Come," he said as he gently tugged her hand upward until she rose stiffly to her feet. "Allow me to give you a tour of my home while the little one sleeps. That way you can see what things my home doesn't have that you will need."

This close, Amber felt just how much heat was radiating off Raphek's body. It made her want to lean closer, to wrap her arms around him and allow his heat to embrace her like a warm blanket. Instead, she carefully pulled her hand from within his and pivoted on her heel to bend over Matty and plant a gentle kiss on his forehead, hoping her actions didn't look totally contrived.

She hoped her hands weren't shaking because inside, she was shaking like a freaking earthquake. Her heart was also beating as though she had just finished running a marathon.

Amber was a bigger mess than even she had thought if a bit of physical warmth made her lose her head enough to almost do something as stupid as hug the first man who had treated her like a human being deserving of respect. Dammit, the last thing she needed to do was make things more awkward between them than they already were!

She turned and forced a small smile. "So, you mentioned a meditation room…"

He nodded slowly. "Follow me."

Amber tried not to let the fact that she couldn't read Raphek's expression in that moment bother her.

She was upset, her scent a strange combination of fear, longing, and anger even though the expression she wore as Raphek showed Amber the room he had given her and Matty to use for sleeping was of polite curiosity.

"Are you sure it's okay to have a toddler anywhere near those?" she said, pointing at the hundreds of books and scrolls displayed within several rows of shelving carved into all the stone walls of the room.

"They aren't one-of-a-kind titles or precious heirlooms passed within my family if that's what you're worried about," Raphek replied. "Both of you are more than welcome to peruse them, but unless you wish to learn Draknar, I doubt either one of you will find any enjoyment from them."

Amber chuckled and a bit of the tension she seemed to always carry noticeably relaxed from her shoulders. "Yeah, Matty doesn't even know how to read English yet." Her eyes roamed the entire circumference of the room and then lingered on the rug with the royal House's crest beneath their feet, her expression thoughtful. "With all the books and this gorgeous rug, this room feels a lot homier than a room inside a mountain has any right to be. If I can get a few of those large cushions like you had in your meditation room when we go out later, then I'd say I could make Matty and me a pretty comfy bed."

Raphek smiled, pleased that his new ward seemed a bit more comfortable with the idea of staying in his home. While he understood well the feeling of not wanting to impose, he hoped it wouldn't be a constant weight on her mind. Her scent immitted way too much anxiety as it was. From the few terrible and rage-inducing antidotes about her past that Briana was able to coax out of her during their meal, what should have been a confusing scent made a horrible kind of sense. Amber needed an environment she would feel was a safe enough place for not only her son, but herself to finally let go of that anxiety.

He would damn sure make his home that place for her as long as she wished it. Raphek, himself, had choked on the acrid taste of anxiety day in and day out for centuries during their war with the Ishkkan and Ansi. He would not wish that mental turmoil on anyone. That a child had been experiencing such fear and anxiety for much of his short life was even more heartbreaking.

"We'll get you a chest for your clothing as well," Raphek said. He smiled sheepishly. "The two in here are filled to their lids with the results of centuries worth of personal pursuits. I daresay I haven't opened that large one in the corner for at least a decade."

Amber's eyes widened. "Centuries…?"

He nodded. "Draknos are long-lived. Me? I'm about 4,900 years old, give or take a decade or two."

"Wait! Wait! You're nearly *five* thousand years old!"

"Elysian years, yes. We've determined that our days as well as years on our home world were a bit longer than their Earth equivalents."

"That's amazing!" Amber said, her tone dripping with awe. "I'm only twenty-three, so I can't even imagine living to a hundred much less for several thousand years. With all the gossip going around about dragons these days, I'm shocked I've never heard you can live so long."

"Few Terrans know this about us. It's not something we've disclosed to even your leaders in Washington, so I would ask that you keep this particular truth to yourself when talking to other Terrans," Raphek said.

"Of course," Amber agreed quickly. "I don't want to get you into any trouble."

Raphek shook his head, annoyed with himself when her anxiety spiked within her scent. "Don't worry. It's not forbidden to speak of such things to Terrans. At the same time, it's probably best we don't telegraph what makes our two peoples different when so many Terrans are still wary of our presence."

"Understandable," she said seriously. "Since you have access to the internet here, I'm sure you've run across at least some of the anti-dragon sentiments making the rounds."

Raphek grimaced. "Unfortunately."

"I'm sorry."

Amber's face was pinched as though she were on the verge of tears.

He tilted his head in confusion. "Whatever for?"

"Because I screwed up, your kingdom now has a huge spotlight pointed at it that you never asked for," she replied bitterly. "I really should have known better than to think I could ask a kingdom for help that had so many eyes already scrutinizing it without anyone finding out."

Amber looked so lost and miserable in that moment that Raphek couldn't help but step closer to her and draw her into a hug, wanting only to comfort her. She instantly stiffened, her heartbeat nearly doubling, and for a horrible second, Raphek thought he had made a grave mistake. Had he just committed a Terran social faux pas? He wasn't as versed in Terran society as his friends, Airon and Sevek were...

Then Amber's entire body seemed to go boneless in his arms as she leaned her head against his chest and wrapped her arms around his waist tightly in return. The sigh that followed was ragged and sounded utterly exhausted.

"I was glad to help you," Raphek said into the thick silence that followed. "I'm even more pleased that I am able to continue helping you and Matty now."

"You can't be real," she muttered into his chest.

Not understanding the underlining emotion threaded within her tone, Raphek merely tightened his arms around her and said nothing. Luckily, she didn't seem to expect an answer if her steadily slowing heartbeat were any indication.

He was beginning to regret not asking more questions about Terran society while socializing with his friends who had Terran mates. Of course, he had never imagined himself acting as a patron to an emotionally wounded young Terran woman and her child, so he really shouldn't be too hard on himself about it. He knew that, but…

Raphek sighed inwardly. At the very least, the anxiety permeating Amber's scent was nowhere near as potent as it had been when they had left Matty sleeping on the couch to tour his home.

"My injured leg is starting to shake," Amber abruptly said as she pulled away from his chest enough to look up at his face with blue eyes that were a bit glassy and reminded him of the jewels that they had been talking about earlier. "I think I should probably go join Matty again on the couch before you have to do something as embarrassing as carry me there."

Her face was flushed, and Raphek couldn't help but think that the color highlighted her pale skin beautifully. He had a sudden desire to run his fingertips across her cheeks and see if her skin was as soft and silky as Airon had once told him was a specific trait of Terran women.

Feeling a bit discomfited, Raphek released his hold on her and took a step back to give her space. At least, that's what he told himself.

"Does the muscle where you were wounded hurt?" he asked.

"Not at all, but Lady Serie did say that I might feel a little weakness in it for the next few days, so…"

Raphek frowned. "Maybe I should wait until tomorrow to take you into the city."

"Oh! It's not that bad," Amber said quickly. "Besides, I think a little exercise would be good for it, and trust me, you don't want a bored three-year-old rampaging about your home. Only his T-rex plushie made it here with him, but that'll only distract him for so long. Emma told me about a few toys that are popular with Draknos children that I can find down in the city."

"I have a tablet that he can watch videos on, as well," Raphek said as they made their way back to the main room.

"Does everyone have one?"

He smiled. "Pretty much. Your movies and TV shows have become extremely popular among my people over the years."

Amber's eyes lit up prettily. "Then have you watched…"

For the next hour, they sat in the main room sipping

cold drinks and had a pleasant conversation about various movies and shows while they waited for Matty to wake up from his nap. He was pleased that they shared a similar taste for detective shows. His best friend, Airon, often teased him about his preference as he had always had a slight—*slight*, mind you—obsession with puzzles of all kinds. Airon had once even brought him a Terran children's toy called a Rubik's Cube that had clearly been meant as a joke, but he had enjoyed solving it immensely.

By the time Matty had awakened and they were ready to go down to the city, nearly all of Amber's anxiety had disappeared from her scent.

And Raphek found he couldn't take his eyes off her.

CHAPTER TEN

Amber felt as though she had entered the marketplace within a fantasy novel as she led Matty by the hand and closely followed Raphek through the crowd of colorfully dressed dragon-shifters and past stalls of unfamiliar foods and items. This area of the dragon city reminded her of an especially large farmer's market that had collided with a flea market. Yet, amidst all that organized chaos, she couldn't believe how relaxed and full of curiosity she felt.

She had been shot only twenty-four hours ago while she had been running with Matty clutched in her arms for their lives for God's sake! She shouldn't be walking around at all with only a hint of fatigue deep in her bones to show for it!

However, that wasn't the most insane part of her whole situation.

Amber couldn't remember the last time since Matty was born that she hadn't been a human ball of anxiety. Not for the first time since they had left Raphek's place, she couldn't help but wonder if she was somehow drunk on the magic Lady Serie had used to heal her yesterday, that it had also somehow taken the sharp edges off all the negative emotions that had been relentlessly bombarding her since leaving Houston. It just seemed inconceivable that a mere show of human—or in this case, dragon—decency from a handful of people could soothe away that kind of constant anxiety.

Even the few visits with her parents that Garrett had allowed her once his true personality had reared its ugly head had been filled with oceans of anxiety that had left her nauseous for the rest of the day because of her worry that she or they would say or do something that Garrett would interpret as either insulting or threatening to his sense of self-importance and lash out—often violently. It was also after those times of imagined slights that the bastard had threatened to use his family connections to ruin her parents both financially and socially because they "need to learn their place."

Garrett's family name and personal reputation were everything to him. Period. End of story.

Amber felt sick to admit it, but it was that fear for her parents, the crushing guilt for being naïve enough to fall for Garrett's initial charm and getting pregnant so young, that had made her just grit her teeth and accept the beatings, no matter how many times her mother had pleaded with her to just take Matty and leave the monster anyway, their business be damned. Then Garrett began to threaten to take Matty away from her if she ever tried to leave him, and thoughts of leaving him had instantly vanished. She had felt so horribly trapped.

She glanced at Raphek walking just a half-step in front of her, feeling something like bewilderment. What was the most inconceivable was that she had not only allowed the dragon-man to hug her but also had allowed herself to just let go of all the worries that were crushing her and bask in his encompassing warmth for one seemingly eternal moment. For the first time in years, she had felt *safe*.

And that was dangerous. Amber knew that. She *knew*, but...

"Feel free to stop anywhere to browse," Raphek said abruptly, looking over his shoulder at her with an encouraging smile. "Matty, too. Especially the fruit stalls."

Amber glanced to her left at a couple of merchant

stalls and eyed the colorful array of what she assumed where Elysian fruits and vegetables. She looked back at Raphek and said a bit sheepishly, "How about you point out some of your favorite foods? Maybe describe how they taste? With my luck, I would pick out all the bitter-tasting foods that Matty would absolutely hate."

Raphek raised an eyebrow. "And you wouldn't?"

"I would hold my breath and swallow every mouthful as though it were the best thing I had ever tasted," Amber admitted.

Raphek chuckled. "We wouldn't want that."

Amber desperately tried to ignore how the sound of his laugh seemed to make her cheeks warm.

"Can we taste one of those red ones?" Matty asked, pointing at a large pile of a plum-sized and blood-red food item arranged in the center of one of the food stalls. She hadn't realized that he had been listening to her and Raphek's conversation.

"You can if you like," Raphek told him affably. "However, though that one may look pretty, it's only really used in soups."

"So, it's a vegetable?" Amber asked.

"I suppose a root would be a better description. It has a bit of a—spicy flavor."

"It's not sweet like an apple, Matty. It's like an onion or a pepper."

Matty pouted. "Oh."

Raphek bent down and told him, "How about I get you one of those big purple ones over there, instead? They're as sweet as sugar." He pointed to a small fruit stand a few feet farther down the stone-cobbled street.

Matty's eyes lit up. "Okay!"

He then did something that had Amber's eyes widening in shock. Matty dropped her hand and grabbed Raphek's, tugging the dragon-man excitedly towards the fruit stand. "Let's go! Let's go!"

It took Amber a moment to pick her jaw off the ground before she hurried after them. Matty was usually shy around adults he didn't know, painfully so around men, especially if they were the loud and boisterous sort.

Come to think of it, both Raphek and Sevek had spent time around Matty yesterday while she had been sleeping off the effects of her healing, and now she was kicking herself for not taking at least Emma aside and asking her a ton of questions about that missing time. Raphek had, of course, talked with and interacted with Matty during their lunch with Princess Briana, but it had been understandably extremely limited. Not nearly enough in her experience for her son to lose his wariness of a stranger.

Had he had a great bit more positive interaction with

him yesterday at Emma's, or was the fact that Matty had seen Raphek turn into a dragon make him not really see their host as a man?

"That looks like a slightly rounder eggplant without the stem or the smooth skin," Amber said, wrinkling her nose as she watched Matty take an enthusiastic bite out of the Elysian fruit. However, unlike eggplant, its insides were exactly the same color as its skin.

"It tastes like grape juice, Mommy," Matty informed her with a purple-stained grin and then took another bite that crunched as though he were biting into an apple.

"Hopefully, it doesn't have seeds like grapes," Amber said, looking up at Raphek worriedly.

"It does, but the seeds are extremely soft—gelatinous, I believe is the English word for their consistency. Completely edible," Raphek assured her.

"Taste it, Mommy," Matty said offering up the large fruit with both hands.

The Rekkan woman that was selling the fruit was watching them with keen eyes. Suddenly feeling as though she were on display, herself, Amber nonetheless accepted the purple fruit and took a tentative bite. Just as a heavy, sweet flavor that did indeed taste remarkably like the grape juice boxes that Matty enjoyed hit her tongue, a squirt of fruit juice also splashed across her chin. A couple of drops had also likely landed onto the front of her borrowed tunic-dress.

And not a wet wipe or napkin in sight, Amber thought with a resigned sigh as she lowered the fruit from her mouth.

However, before she could wipe her chin with the back of her free hand, Raphek reached over and swiped a thumb firmly across her chin. "I think I got all of it."

As Amber stood frozen at the unexpected touch, Raphek licked the juice off his thumb in a slow slide that suddenly had her blood heating up and her heart racing. The smile he flashed her afterward was so innocent that Amber immediately distrusted it. Then again—he *couldn't* have meant that the way her treacherous body had interpreted it. Could he?

Aware that more than the eyes of the fruit seller were watching, Amber forced a benign smile onto her lips instead of continuing to freak out inside and said in a tone she prayed was normal, "Thanks."

Yeah, the best course of action would be to continue on their little shopping excursion and pretend nothing out of the ordinary had happened.

At all.

So why the hell couldn't she calm down her racing heart?

CHAPTER ELEVEN

She was blushing again.

Raphek had no idea what had caused that delightful reaction in Amber this time, but it had been happening on and off, sometimes with only a mere glance from him, all afternoon. He really wanted to pause and take in that loveliness at his leisure that had fascinated him since the first time he had witnessed it in front of the fruit stand, but laden down as he was with the afternoon's purchases as they headed for the lifts, it was unfortunately an inopportune time. Plus, Matty's scent had begun to exhibit a bit of tiredness, and the last thing he wanted was to cause the poor child a prolonging of his discomfort because of Raphek's own whims.

Besides, he had already indulged his curiosity about the softness of Amber's skin earlier when a splash of fruit juice on her chin had given him the perfect excuse, and that had resulted in a maelstrom of scents emanating from her that had made him instantly feel both guilty and then thoughtful.

Arousal.

That sweet smell had been practically screaming at him as had her suddenly racing heartbeat, completely unexpected and startling. His own senses may have even responded in similar fashion to such blatant interest from an attractive female had another scent just beneath that arousal and just as potent not arisen to slap him hard in the nose as though in admonishment.

Anxiety—and a hint of fear.

Yet, she had smiled at him with a calm expression and had continued perusing the food stalls as though her emotions weren't in turmoil. Raphek had expected her to put a bit of distance between them in an effort to find her mental equilibrium again, but then the surreptitious glances at him had started, mostly when they were walking between merchant stalls. Sometimes, she would blush after a glance, and other times, her scent would spike briefly with arousal.

However, never once did the acrid scent of anxiety fade even a little bit from her scent.

His own worry and guilt about that made him consider his own reactions more closely. Relationships had never been on the forefront of his mind even when he had first come of age. His friends had always teased him about his seeming reticence regarding courting as him simply holding out for his fated mate. No matter how many times he had rolled his eyes at the accusation, the ribbing continued to this day.

Admittedly, Raphek had enjoyed carrying out a bit of teasing of his own when both Airon and Sevek had sworn that fated mates were real, and even more astonishingly, that they had found their fated mates, each claiming one of two human sisters. It was only fair.

How ironic that he now found himself undoubtably attracted to this golden-haired, wounded human woman who blushed so beautifully. His interest wasn't anything like the all-encompassing need to claim like Airon had described had awakened within him upon meeting Lillian, but it *was* there. It had been there ever since they had chatted away in his sitting room while they had waited for Matty to awaken. Maybe it was as simple as compatible personalities or even just the fact that he found the way her emotions came alive through her facial expressions more fascinating than he had anything else in a long while.

The only question now was whether or not it was

wise to let Amber know that her interest in him had been noticed and was welcome, especially when she seemed troubled by that attraction. From what Raphek understood, human marriages were nowhere near as binding as a Bonding of Fire was for the Rekkan. Amber, herself, had expressed to Briana that it had been her desire to permanently dissolve her marriage to Garrett Johnson from the moment the abuse had started but had been prevented from doing so because of the Terran vermin's threats. That desire was one of the reasons why Amber had rather adamantly asked the princess to continue using her maiden name "Davis" for both her and Matty while they were within the kingdom.

She need not have worried. As far as Raphek and Elysia South as a whole were concerned, Amber was free to pursue any amorous interests to her heart's desire as Terran contracts meant nothing here. Maybe Briana's agreement to honor her wish hadn't made that fact clear to Amber. If so, then it was no wonder that she seemed so conflicted by her attraction to him.

Or—her anxiety could stem from a reason he, as a Draknos, couldn't possibly fathom. How many times had he watched a Terran movie or TV show where a Terran character's actions had been completely incomprehensible? Thus, it would be the epitome of arrogance to think he understood Terrans from watching their fictional stories or his brief social interactions with three Terran women.

Raphek suddenly lamented the absence of his best friend and his rather blunt advice, but Airon wasn't due to report to the king for another couple of weeks. Maybe Sevek would—

He was instantly drawn out of his thoughts at the sight of one of his guards-brothers that was normally assigned to the king's Guard standing directly in his path in the center of the lift chamber. Eosien was wearing an alarmingly dire expression.

"Trouble?" Raphek asked when he reached the other.

Eosien's eyes glanced briefly at Briana before replying in Draknar, *"Apparently, a Terran senator is currently raising a ruckus regarding your Terran ward over various Terran medias. The king wishes to see you both in the council chamber with all haste."*

A growl threatened to rise from his throat, but Raphek managed to keep it behind his teeth. He was keenly aware of Matty staring up at him, and he didn't want to inadvertently scare the boy.

"Do me a favor and deliver these to my home, and much thanks," Raphek said, thrusting their purchases into Eosien's hands.

Eosien nodded. *"Of course, guards-brother."*

Raphek turned to Amber. "A problem regarding Senator Johnson has just arisen. The king is waiting for us."

Amber's wary expression instantly turned to one of alarm as fear inundated her scent. "What happened?"

He shook his head. "We'll soon find out." He glanced down at Matty and frowned. "I know the little one is tired. I would suggest leaving him with Emma, but she's currently teaching a class."

"Emma's probably the only one he would stay with right now," Amber agreed as she picked up Matty and balanced him onto her hip. "He had a pretty long nap earlier, so I think he'll be fine."

They hurried to the royals' designated lift and were outside the council chamber within minutes. The smell of Amber's fear hadn't lessened a bit. It awakened his protective instincts a thousand-fold. He wanted nothing more than to draw them both into the fold of his arms and growl in warning to any who approached. Instead, he grit his teeth and settled on placing a hand gently onto Amber's shoulder as he guided her into the chamber once they had been announced.

Seated at the head of the long conference table was, of course, the king. Four of the other seats were taken by Queen Izot, Prince Ansel, Prince Astaron, and Princess Briana. All of them had a tablet resting on a stand before them. Things really must be dire for all these royals to be present.

Raphek bowed deeply to them, and Amber hastily dipped her head as well. She was visibly trembling.

"I'm glad Eosien was able to locate you so quickly. Please, sit," the queen said, gesturing to a couple of empty seats next to Briana.

"Thank you, Your Highness," Raphek said.

He pulled out a seat for Amber and Matty before he took the one next to Briana. Amber's anxiety was almost tangible, but she still offered the royals a quiet "thank you" as well before she sat, Matty once again hiding his face in his mother's chest in the face of so many new strangers.

Raphek caught the king's eye. At the monarch's nod, Raphek handled the introductions. "Amber, may I present His Majesty, King Dagon, Her Majesty, Queen Izot, their son, Crown Prince Ansel, and King Dagon's brother, Prince Astaron. You, of course, have already met Prince Astaron's mate, Princess Briana. All are of the Rekkan royal House of the Red Flame."

"Amber Davis," Amber greeted, her voice still tinged with nerves. "This is my son, Matthew. Um—thank you so much for allowing us sanctuary in your kingdom, Your Majesties. Considering..."

Queen Izot offered Amber a radiant smile. "We are

always pleased when we can offer aid wherever we can." Her lips then thinned with displeasure. "Unfortunately, there are those who will always try to exploit the kindness of others, as well."

"Which brings us to our current predicament," Dagon said. "Along with your efforts, Raphek, Ansel and Lyven have also been keeping an eye on various Terran social media sites for me regarding that nasty business at our border yesterday. Briana, why don't you show them the video, and let Senator Johnson speak for himself."

Amber stiffened as the princess turned the stand of her tablet until the screen faced them. A Terran man with brown hair threaded with silver and dressed in a dark blue suit Raphek had often seen Terran men in power wear stood behind a podium. Both the US flag and the Texas flag were displayed prominently behind him. His face was frozen in a rather stern expression, his eyes narrowed and mouth opened as though in mid-bellow.

Senator Johnson looked a bit older than the official headshot Raphek had seen on the man's website.

Briana tapped the play icon, and Senator Johnson began to speak rather animatedly. The moment the man's booming voice filled the room, a burst of fear appeared in Matty's scent. Raphek's eyes briefly slanted worriedly towards his wards in enough time to see the little boy try to burrow even deeper into Amber's chest.

A surge of anger rose within him. Raphek wondered if Matty had also experienced violence at the hands of the senator if just hearing the despicable man's voice caused such a negative reaction. It was a question he would definitely need to ask Amber later when they were alone.

Amber's face seemed almost a blank mask. Luckily, her scent filled with equal parts fear, anger, and disgust told him the real story.

"That's Houston's Chief of Police standing off to the side," Amber said in a strained voice.

Raphek's attention focused once again on the video and the senator's words. His eyebrows rose with every sentence.

"Missing? *That's* the story he's going with?" He looked over at the king. "I must admit, Your Majesty, I expected you to tell me that the senator had leaked the type of video we had discussed yesterday of me snatching Amber and Matty through the energy shield and the condemnation of dragons had begun."

"Oh, I'm sure that's coming, and soon," Dagon said dryly.

Movement in the corner of his eye had Raphek looking back down at the tablet. A photo of a smiling Amber holding an equally grinning Matty in a Terran home had appeared on the screen.

Amber gasped. "That's a picture that my Mom took of us…" she said, her voice dripping with anguish.

"One that Senator Johnson should not possess?" Raphek guessed.

"No." Amber's answer was barely a whisper.

"I know you told me that you were afraid your husband's family would hurt your parents in retaliation," Briana said grimly, "but I don't think he's done anything nefarious to them yet."

"Not that I've seen," Ansel seconded as he looked up from his own screen and offered Amber a reassuring smile. "The story is blowing up on AlwaysChat right now, and so far, I haven't seen any chatter concerning your parents. Nor did I see their names mentioned anywhere in the Houston media before the senator's news conference. No mention of dragons or Elysia South, either."

"Yet," Amber insisted miserably, hugging Matty more tightly. "I know Senator Johnson. He doesn't have one compassionate bone in his body. It may seem like he's doing this because he cares for his son, but he cares about Garrett—and as an extension, Matty—only so far as a tool for continuing the family line, tools that *will not* be allowed to tarnish the Johnson family name at all costs." She took a deep, ragged breath, and then firmed her lips, a look of resolve darkening her eyes as she fixed them on the king. "That's why I'll leave Elysia South right now, before he can sully the Rekkan's reputation."

CHAPTER TWELVE

"There's no way that I will allow you to walk willingly to your death," Raphek growled, "to allow Matty to fall back into the hands of a creature that would purposely harm a child."

This time, Amber was sure she saw red flames ignite in his eyes. She shook herself mentally. She couldn't allow herself to become distracted by her completely inappropriate attraction to him as she undoubtably had all afternoon, no matter how mesmerizing and beautiful his sudden manifestation of real dragon fire made him.

"I don't plan to go back to Houston," she insisted. "I'll just run again. Head north for a few hours until I reach a small town like Gordonville or Sherwood Shores then borrow someone's cell phone to call the Houston PD to let them know that I'm not missing, that Garrett knows very well why I took Matty and left him. I'll mention my plans to file for divorce and that I'll have my lawyer call him."

"On foot and with no money?" Briana interjected skeptically. "With a three-year-old in tow? Both those towns are dozens of miles away! As you well saw today during your excursion into our city, we don't exactly have a car we can loan you were we even thus inclined to allow you to do such a rash thing."

But I do have money—sort of, Amber thought, an image of her wedding ring flashing through her head. That she might need a lot of cash fast was one of the main reasons she didn't leave it behind. All she would need to do is find a pawn shop.

"I *won't* allow those monsters to play games with the lives of your people. Nor with Matty's." Amber turned her gaze to the two monarchs at the head of the table, suddenly feeling nauseous because of what she was about to do, what she had prayed she would never have to do. "It was beyond selfish for me to come seeking asylum with you in the first place, but even so, Raphek saved us without hesitation. You took us in. We've been shown so much kindness from everyone here despite the huge political problems Matty and I represent. I want to repay that kindness; I *can* repay that kindness by drawing everyone's eyes away from here, put a wrench in whatever the senator is cooking up. But—" Amber forced the rest out, feeling as though she were brutally stabbing herself in the heart. "—Matty doesn't have to be with me when I do it."

Raphek drew in a sharp breath.

"Then Raphek will be accompanying you," King Dagon said calmly into the shocked silence before anyone else could speak, the heat in his eyes practically daring her to argue. "He will then bring you back as soon as your task is complete."

Beside her, Raphek visibly relaxed. "Yes," he agreed firmly.

"That could work," Prince Astaron chimed in, sharing a look with Briana that Amber couldn't quite decipher.

"Being seen with you kind of defeats the purpose of me trying to show that dragons had nothing to do with my disappearance," Amber protested. "Your eyes are a dead giveaway!"

"I won't be seen," Raphek said confidently.

"But—"

"We also won't be walking," he cut in with a satisfied smile.

It was Amber's turn to gasp. "You can't fly outside your borders! You could be shot down!"

"Tonight's a new moon. Your military's radar cannot

detect us. As long as we fly during the night and fly high, no one will see me," Raphek said. "I'll land right at the edge of whatever town you choose, shift into my human form, and follow you from the shadows until you can find a convenience store or the like. The store clerk is bound to have a phone you can borrow."

"Yes, somewhere with security cameras would be best," Briana said. "Also, rather than a small town here in Texas, you should fly to one in Oklahoma."

"I'll look for a suitable one," Ansel offered.

Amber shook her head. "The cameras won't matter. Garrett's father will just confiscate the footage, anyway, once the phone call is traced to the area."

"The princess is right, though. At the very least, it's best someone working in a public place sees you," Raphek insisted. "Sometimes, gossip can be a good thing."

"Hopefully, several someones," King Dagon added. "I don't for a moment doubt that some kind of footage from your attack at our border will make its way onto the internet even after you assure the Houston authorities of your wellbeing. Henry Johnson, after all, isn't someone unknown to me. Far from it."

Amber's stomach sank to the bottom of her feet with a sense of dread. "How so?"

The king bared his teeth in obvious disgust. It

painted a very alarming picture that made the hairs at the back of her neck stand up, and Amber was at once relieved that his ire wasn't directed at her. It was the first time she had seen him be anything less than the serene monarch and made her realize that once again, her dangerous penchant for unconsciously judging people as benign based on a first impression had reared its ugly head again.

This was a dangerous man who had the ability to reign fire down on cities from his very mouth. As was Raphek, though her patron made it very easy for her to forget with his genuine kindness.

"Johnson is one of a handful of anti-dragon senators that have caused me quite a few headaches over the years," King Dagon explained in a more even tone than Amber had expected. "They pretend that they are concerned for their constituents' safety, but after researching their backgrounds, it's obvious that it's their own bank accounts and the possibility of losing them that truly is behind their enmity of both the Rekkan and Ishkkan."

With every word, Amber's sense of dread increased. "Senator Johnson is an oil baron. Did Elysia South bring a huge oil reservoir when your land appeared here from your world or something?"

"No, nothing as straightforward as that. Just as with

every world leader around the world, it's our energy shields that have them fixated. While others see a powerful source of clean energy they hope to one day replicate, Senator Johnson and his ilk only see it as a threat to the future viability of his company."

"And a threat to his power," Amber added grimly.

"That truth already placed me in a very precarious position," King Dagon said. "I'm sure Raphek has told you that Draknos view children as our greatest treasures, so saving you and your son was something that every one of my people would have done without hesitation. There is *nothing* to regret. If it hadn't been today, then it would have been tomorrow. Vermin always find a way to cause chaos. However, we have now handed our adversaries in Washington a very powerful weapon in the form of video evidence of a firedrake breaking Terran law, at the very least. Add to that the narrative he spun today about a missing daughter-in-law and grandson, and suddenly, any footage from the incident can be made to look like an abduction.

"Thus, Miss Davis, any way you can instill doubt in whatever nefarious way the senator will present the footage to the Terran public will make any future denial on my part to the Terran powers that be that you and your son are still within my kingdom more plausible. I can no longer afford to allow Washington to make the next move on this matter. We must go on the offensive." He paused and swept the entire room with his eyes. "All of us."

Amber bit her lip. She could well imagine the panic that would ensue if people suddenly thought the dragons were stealing women and children to hoard behind their impenetrable shields. No, not only thought but had "proof" they could see over and over with their own eyes. She, herself, had allowed only *rumors* to lead her to that dragon-viewing platform yesterday because she had been so desperate and afraid. Fear might have the military dropping bombs on the four Elysias again.

Was she seriously going to allow the dragons to continue to stick their necks out for her with *that* very probable threat hanging over their heads? To agree to Raphek's help? When it was so dangerous *right now*, not just for Raphek, but for the Rekkan as a whole if a dragon were spotted illegally flying over Oklahoma before any public opinion had been turned against the dragons because of her asshole father-in-law's greed and lust for power?

A heavy sigh had her instantly looking down at Matty. Somehow, the poor boy had managed to fall asleep sometime after they had watched the news conference even as hearing his grandfather's voice had distressed him as it always did. He looked so peaceful—

and the devastating thought of Matty waking up and being told that his Mommy was never coming back decided her.

"And you'll take care of Matty while Raphek and I are outside of the kingdom?" Amber asked King Dagon anxiously.

The king's eyes softened. "Of course."

"Matty can stay with Emma and Sevek again," Raphek assured her. "It's best he stays with people that are familiar."

Amber's hands tightened involuntarily on Matty. "Yeah."

Could this revised version of her hastily blurted out plan actually help to muddy the waters enough to prevent permanently damaging all the goodwill in people's minds that the Draknos had established over the past four years? Senator Johnson knew for a fact that Amber and Matty had been taken into Elysia South. King Dagon was right. There was no way the bastard wouldn't try to use that fact against everyone to achieve his desired outcome.

Her monster of a father-in-law had done it before the first and only time Amber had tried to leave Garrett after he had punched her so hard in the face that she had blacked out during a fit of rage after losing his first political race. Her parents' business had barely survived the prelude to the ultimatum Henry Johnson had given her.

Amber's initial intentions before the king had nixed the idea of her leaving the kingdom alone had been to follow her Plan B, to lay a trail of breadcrumbs in various towns and cities leading towards the Canadian border for Garrett and his father to chase and then try to disappear in some little town in Montana or something. Breadcrumbs in the form of phone calls along the way to a divorce lawyer she had secretly contacted with the help of the same friend who had secured her a car for their escape right before they had left Houston as part of that Plan B in case she had failed to gain sanctuary in Elysia South. Plan B had been convoluted, and she hated to admit it, just as likely to have failed as her ludicrous hopes to talk a dragon into letting Matty and her illegally into his kingdom.

Guilt once again threatened to crush her until she couldn't breathe as she looked at Raphek.

She prayed with everything within her that she hadn't just signed this beautiful, kind dragon-shifter's death warrant by accepting his help. King Dagon may believe that this whole mess with Senator Johnson was inevitable, but that didn't mean that Amber was any less deserving of the blame for being the catalyst that had set that inevitability in motion.

She *had* to fix this. No matter what.

Raphek, ever the gentleman, offered to carry Matty to Emma's. As Amber watched how tenderly the dragon-man cradled her son in his arms, she couldn't help but feel a sense of relief that should the worst happen while they were in Oklahoma and she were killed, then Matty would be in the best hands with Raphek as his guardian.

CHAPTER THIRTEEN

Amber held onto the bundle of Raphek's clothing more tightly than was necessary as she sat protected within his enormous dragon hands and gazed anxiously between the gaps in his fingers. It was so dark that she couldn't see a thing, making her feel even more uneasy about the whole endeavor.

All she knew—and only because Raphek had told her—was that they had just flown over the Red River and were now somewhere in the middle of nowhere in Oklahoma. Admittedly, Amber would have been feeling much more freaked out at the moment if they had not traveled through a secret underground tunnel out of Elysia South that had told her without words that the Rekkan had likely been soaring the Texas skies from day one with none being the wiser.

That King Dagon had allowed Raphek to reveal such a colossal secret to her made her think that the firedrake king expected her and Matty to remain in Elysia South indefinitely. The thought made her feel both relief and sadness. If she remained with the firedrakes, then she wondered if she would ever get to see her parents in person again, secret tunnel or no secret tunnel. She and Matty were simply too much of a political risk for the Rekkan, and nothing short of the death of the entire Johnson family would change that no matter how much she wished it were different.

Ultimately, they had decided on the small town of Kingston out of all the options Prince Ansel had offered them. The thought of a prince, an heir to a real throne in a kingdom that functioned as a true monarchy, doing such a normal task as looking up towns on a map app was really surreal. If not for all the bowing and use of titles, it was easy to forget that the royals were royals.

It was also surreal that she and Matty were now being taken care of by a royal family.

Figures that she was also really attracted to a member of said royal family, even if Raphek was from a more distant branch than the king. That she seemed to gravitate to men with complicated families was the very reason she was up the shit creek as badly as she currently was.

Even though you may consider yourself divorced from Garrett in your heart, this is absolutely the worst *time to be lusting after another man, no matter how gorgeous and great with Matty he is!*

"We're about five minutes from the outskirts of Kingston," Raphek's voice suddenly boomed, saving her from a rapidly downward spiral of self-deprecating admonishments. "There's a sizeable copse of trees bisected by railroad tracks near a main street where the convenience store is located. You'll be approaching from the back of the store, so the property's entrance on that side will be unpaved. There's enough open land to the right of the copse that you won't have to risk crossing through anyone's yard. You won't have to walk far— only a few hundred feet."

"I can't fathom how you can see all of that from so far away, much less in the dark!"

"Dragon eyes have a vision range that's pretty much telescopic," he said seriously. "I'll also be able to hear you whisper as well as your heartbeat even while you're inside the convenience store, so if you run into any kind of trouble, I'll know immediately."

"I really, *really* hope we don't get a chance to test that claim."

Even just thinking about all the trouble she could find made Amber's heart already start to race with trepidation, and they hadn't even landed yet! They had picked Kingston because it only had about a thousand or so people, but she still dreaded having to walk around in public. Was she already suffering from PTSD from getting shot yesterday or did her fear stem from her usual paranoia?

God, she really hoped that she wouldn't have a panic attack inside that convenience store. Matty, her parents, and the firedrakes were counting on her succeeding in throwing this big wrench into the senator's plans.

After they landed, Amber spent a few minutes walking around in a small circle to stretch her legs, pointedly not looking in Raphek's direction as he shifted back into a man and dressed. Seeing Raphek nude would *not* help matters at all right now. Her heart was pounding enough as it was.

"I've never worn jeans before," Raphek said, making Amber automatically look over at him before she could stop herself.

She caught a glimpse of his six-pack abs as he finished pulling the hem of his black T-shirt down over them. Just as she had suspected after allowing him to hold her in his arms while she had fallen apart in the room that was to be her and Matty's bedroom, the man was ripped. He filled out that T-shirt damned well—and yeah, she really should stop ogling him before she started drooling.

Thinking about her attraction to the dragon-man was utterly the wrong thing to distract her from how freaking scared she was about what she was about to do. Her mind needed to be *clear*.

Raphek plucked at the thick, black material experimentally. "I thought they would be uncomfortable, but they're surprisingly more flexible and roomier than I expected."

"Yeah, I'm glad I fit into a pair of Emma's," Amber said. "At any rate, we now both look sufficiently Terran —as long no one sees your eyes in the light."

"I'll be careful," he promised.

Raphek then paused and stared over at her with an unreadable expression for a long, uncomfortable moment that sent her heart into overdrive. He then stepped closer to her until their shoes were practically touching and very deliberately reached down to gently cup her face between his scorching hands, his eyes suddenly glowing—yes, they really were freaking *glowing*—an eerie red.

Amber's lips parted in a soft gasp, but before she could say anything, Raphek bent down and claimed her mouth with lips that made her feel as though she were kissing the sun. She gasped again in complete shock as an equally hot tongue swiped into her mouth for a sole sensual caress against her own before Raphek withdrew both lips and tongue completely.

"Make sure you stay as safe as possible after you leave my side, and I'll give you an even better kiss when you come back to me," Raphek promised in a tone so gravely serious that Amber, at first, thought her now short-circuiting brain had heard him wrong.

Amber had to clutch at his forearms to steady herself, her mind going a million-miles-a-second. What in the world had just happened?

"R-Raphek…?"

He offered her one of his signature gentle smiles and bent down to kiss her forehead tenderly. He then drew his hands away from her cheeks, and Amber immediately missed their warmth even though she was confused as hell.

"Draknos have an excellent sense of smell," he said. "I just suddenly felt the need to give you an answer to what my nose has been picking up from you all afternoon."

"All Draknos have noses better than a bloodhound. Remember that."

Princess Briana's offhand warning suddenly echoed

loudly in her mind as her cheeks seemingly burst into flames. Was he insinuating that he could *smell* her attraction to him?

"Oh."

Amber mentally cringed. That was certainly a lame response, but how the hell was she supposed to respond to something so crazy? To something so—fantastic.

She stepped forward and let her forehead fall onto his chest with a sigh. God, she really was hopeless, wasn't she?

Amber lifted her head and smiled shyly. "Another kiss. That really is quite the incentive."

"Good."

She reluctantly stepped away from his warmth and then turned on her heel without another word, afraid that she wouldn't be able to leave if she looked at him for a second longer.

The walk through the weeds quickly robbed her of the pleasant tingling on her lips Raphek's kiss had left her only to replace that unexpected bit of pleasantness with what felt like a cold rock full of sharp edges in the pit of her stomach. It didn't help her nerves that the whole time, Amber could clearly see the illuminated convenience store like a bright monster that was way closer than she would have liked.

She forced herself not to drag her feet. *The sooner you get there, the sooner you can hopefully find someone to lend you a phone, and the sooner you and Raphek can fly back to Elysia South and Matty.*

Amber refused to think about the promised kiss.

A white pickup truck was the only vehicle to pass her before Amber crossed the road directly to the gravel road that curved around the right side of the store to the paved parking lot in the front. Her heart twisted painfully with more nerves when she rounded the corner and immediately saw two vehicles parked out front, a black sedan and a pickup truck so dusty that you almost couldn't tell it was white.

Remember, the more people who see my face, the better.

Taking one last deep breath to steady herself, Amber squared her shoulders and marched into the store as casually as she could manage. A quick glance around the inside revealed a middle-aged woman perusing the drink selections in the coolers at the back and what looked like a teenaged boy grabbing a bag of chips. The only other person was the fifty-something man at the register.

Amber made a beeline to the register. "Hi. I'm traveling, and I think my son left my cell phone in a restaurant bathroom a few towns back. I just heard the most absurd news about us on the radio, so could I please borrow your cell phone to call down to Houston?"

"On the radio, you say?" the clerk asked, his eyes curious.

"Yeah. My father-in-law is a jerk of a senator who needs to stay out of my marriage," Amber rushed out, real irritation easily creeping into her tone. Talking about Henry always had left a bad taste in her mouth.

The man's eyes suddenly sharpened. "Wait a minute—there was some brouhaha about a missing woman from Texas on the six o'clock news."

Amber made an angry noise. "Yeah, that was about me. What do you think?" She rolled her eyes. "Do I look like I'm missing?"

The clerk barked a laugh and felt some of her rising tension melt away. He reached into the front pocket of his jeans and pulled out a phone. "Take as long as you need, Miss," he said with a wide grin as he offered her the phone.

"Thank you so much, Sir."

Amber turned on her heel to step away and allow the others in line behind her to check out. She was frightfully startled when she unexpectedly met the hard gaze of a middle-aged, blond-haired man dressed in jeans with what looked like oil stains and a standard, button-up uniform shirt that was equally stained. A mechanic, probably. She hadn't heard anyone else come into the store. Had he been in the bathroom? Dammit, she really needed to pay closer attention to her surroundings!

Amber swallowed thickly and nodded politely to the man even though every instinct within her urged her to run for the hills. "Excuse me."

She could feel his eyes on her as she stepped farther away to the side and a bit into the open section that allowed the employees to step behind the counter, but she dared not check. Amber hurriedly pulled out the slip of paper with the phone number to the Houston PD scribbled on it she had stuffed into one of her front pockets.

With the way her heart was pounding relentlessly, Amber suddenly remembered Raphek's boast about being able to hear her heartbeat even with hundreds of yards and the walls of a building separating them. Crap. Would he think her heart was racing because she was scared and in trouble?

"I'm okay, just startled," Amber muttered so far under her breath that it was nearly inaudible.

She was still a bit skeptical about his claims, but it made her feel better to have done it, regardless.

When her call connected, Amber was instantly put

on hold before she could even speak a word. She waited, tied up in knots and feeling more and more nauseous for what felt like an eternity but was in actuality only about five minutes. She was so wound up that she actually jumped and nearly dropped the phone when the same woman's voice abruptly spoke into her ear.

"Yes, hi, this is Amber Davis Johnson, Senator Johnson's daughter-in-law," she said as steadily as she could. "I just found out that everyone thinks my son Matty and I are missing, and I just want to clear up this huge misunderstanding."

She was suddenly interrupted by a hasty "please hold," and Amber was suddenly afraid that the woman was about to hang up on her because she thought Amber was a fake caller just trolling them.

When the line was finally picked up again, a male voice said gruffly, "This is Special Agent Jones of the Federal Bureau of Investigation. I understand that I am speaking to Amber Johnson."

Amber stiffened. She should have expected it, but yikes. Now she was ten times as nervous.

"Yes, I'm Amber Johnson. I can give you my social as proof if you like, as well as my son's."

At Agent Jones's affirmative, she rattled off both numbers without hesitation.

"Where are you now?" the agent asked.

And there it was, the dreaded question.

"I'd rather not say except that a friend is helping me get into a women's shelter for women who have suffered domestic abuse. What I can say is that I'm in the process of filing for divorce from my husband, Garrett Johnson who is Senator Henry Johnson's only son, and I left him yesterday before the papers could be served because I felt my son and I were no longer safe in that house after he struck my son in the face hard enough to make him bleed from the mouth. I think Garrett must have lied to his father about what happened in the hope of locating us because I can't for the life of me figure out how else today's press conference could've come about. The Johnsons usually shy away from that kind of negative publicity as you can well imagine."

"Did you report the assault of your son?" She could practically hear the skepticism drip from his voice.

"I've tried reporting my husband for assault before," Amber said with real bitterness, "but he's a *Johnson*. It all just got quietly swept under the rug. I doubt you'll even find a record of it. I was warned against ever doing it again. You do the math."

"Even so, I think it's best you and your son return to Houston right away. There are a lot of worried people here," Agent Jones said in a gentle, coaxing voice that immediately raised her hackles.

"I'll be in touch with Garrett once I've consulted with my lawyer. Along with divorce papers, I'll also be filing an Order of Protection against him. I have evidence of Matty's assault."

Amber hung up before the agent could speak again.

CHAPTER FOURTEEN

*A*mber had to pause and breathe deeply several times before she felt calm enough to speak to the convenience store clerk again. She was relieved to see that the creepy guy from before had already left. Only she and the clerk remained.

"Thanks for letting me borrow your phone," Amber said sincerely as she handed it back to the man.

"Couldn't help but overhear," he said apologetically, "but are you going to be okay? There's a motel just a couple of blocks or so due west along this same road with decent rates if you would rather not drive through the night."

She smiled. "I appreciate the heads up. Thanks again."

Just as she pushed open the glass door and stepped

out, Amber saw a familiar, dirty white pickup truck still parked in the same slot up front. She froze.

"I heard there was a big reward for information about you," a deep voice abruptly said *way* too close beside her. "A senator's daughter, was it?"

Amber whirled around so fast that she almost lost her balance, her heart practically choking her throat. Creepy Mechanic Guy stood grinning at her just as creepily as his staring in the checkout line had been. Was she some freaking magnet for trouble? Either that, or the universe really hated her, the bastard.

"Given that I just called and spoke with the Houston PD myself and cleared up the misunderstanding, if a reward was really offered, then that offer is obviously no longer valid," Amber said with what she hoped was a nonchalant shrug. "Plus, the senator isn't my father, thank goodness."

Dammit! Should she go back into the convenience store and ask the old clerk for help or try to make a run for it towards the back of the building? In that split-second of indecision, the man reached out quick as lightning and roughly grabbed her arm in an iron grip.

A sharp pain awakened in her arm as memories of Garrett doing the same countless times, of the bruises in the shape of fingers she *still* had on her arms from the last time he had cruelly manhandled her invaded her mind, and Amber promptly panicked. With a strangled sound that barely resembled anything human, she kicked the bastard hard in the crotch with no thought of who might see her and took off running the second she felt his callused fingers loosen in reaction enough to wrench her arm out of his grip.

Amber sprinted around the building as if the Devil, himself, were after her, and right before she reached the road, she heard footsteps pounding almost preternaturally loud in the gravel behind her. Luckily, she was in a small town, and there was no traffic to worry about this late at night.

She zipped across without bothering to look both ways, back into the weeds of the empty stretch of land she had traversed earlier just as the mechanic snarled between labored breaths, "The hell I'm gonna...let you screw me out of...that reward money, bitch!"

Somehow, Amber found a reservoir of strength that added speed to her legs. She had no doubt this furious man would drag her back across the street to his vehicle by the hair if he had to. It made her wonder exactly how much her asshole father-in-law had offered up as a reward—if the whole damned thing wasn't just a rumor in the first place.

She had barely made it into the cover of the trees when Amber was suddenly grabbed around the waist by an arm as firm as a thick tree limb and a hand firmly placed over her mouth before she could cry out in shock. It took her panicked brain another few seconds before the unusual heat of the hand covering her mouth told her exactly who was currently bearing her away deep into the darkness behind a huge clump of trees and brush.

Raphek...

Once again, she had been saved from a maniac chasing her by a dragon. How embarrassing was that? She *hated* thinking of herself as a damsel in distress.

About thirty seconds later, Creepy Mechanic Guy barreled past the area where they were hiding like a rampaging grizzly bear, panting harshly and cursing. They both stood virtually frozen for a few more tense minutes listening to the sounds of her pursuer crashing through the underbrush become fainter and fainter, Amber tightly pressed against a warm, muscled torso and barely daring to breathe. When only the rustling of tree branches and dead leaves in the slight breeze and Raphek's even breaths behind her were all her puny human ears could detect, Raphek finally removed his hand from over her mouth and released his hold on her waist.

"He's gone back across the street," Raphek said softly as Amber turned around to face him. He reached over and cupped her cheek, rubbing his thumb soothingly over her cheek. "Sorry for the scare. Truly. I saw you coming, and you had enough of a lead on that piece of scum that I thought waiting for you to enter the trees before I made my move was the best option."

"Better *you* scare me than some unknown thug hiding in the trees," Amber said with a shiver. "Good thing you dragons have such telltale high body temperatures, or I might have given you the same treatment as Creepy Mechanic Guy. So, you heard everything, then?"

"Yes. Another fool motivated to harm another by the promise of money. He reeks of motor oil, so he'll be easy for me to evade him should he intend to continue his hunt for you." He snorted disdainfully. "Let him hunt for you until dawn. We'll be safely within Elysia South in less than an hour."

Amber looked around anxiously. "But is it even safe for you to shift and launch into the sky from here? What if he's still watching this area? What if he plans to watch all night? You said it, yourself. People will go to insane lengths for a heap of money."

"He is currently entering a vehicle," Raphek said. "We'll wait here until I can discern where he is going. In the meantime, I do believe I owe you a kiss."

"Does *nothing* rattle you dragons?" Amber muttered, sure her face had instantly reddened. She was seriously going to OD on adrenaline after the myriad of ways her emotions had been jolted in just the past half hour.

Raphek once again drew her into his arms. She let him.

"I've lived a long time."

"That doesn't answer—*mmph!*"

What had she been about to say? Suddenly, all Amber could think about was the silky warmth of the plush lips utterly devouring her own in the type of kiss that she only thought happened in the movies. Raphek's tongue licked teasingly along the seam of her lips, and she parted them without hesitation. The feel of his tongue sliding almost lazily along her own was positively decadent, and Amber couldn't help but moan as a rush of arousal washed through her body and awakened a throbbing in the core of her sex that was in no way appropriate while standing in a thicket of random trees in Oklahoma.

By the time Raphek pulled away, Amber's head was spinning, and she swore that Raphek had been determined to suck every inch of breath from her lungs.

"There it is," he said with a satisfied smile, "that beautiful blush I so adore."

Well—he pretty much just ensured that her cheeks would stay flushed for the rest of the night. She could practically feel him caressing her face with his eyeballs, something she was not at all used to experiencing.

"How can you even see anything? It's nearly pitch black out here!" Amber exclaimed, embarrassed at how breathless she sounded.

How in the hell had she gone from running away from some rando to being kissed within an inch of her life by a dragon-shifter in less than ten minutes? She should be freaking out about Henry involving the FBI and the fact that the whole country now knew her face, not swooning over a gorgeous man like a love-starved idiot without a care in the world! That said gorgeous man treated their abrupt change in relationship so matter-of-factly without a hint of hesitation didn't help her sense of unreality at all!

"Not for a dragon's eyes," Raphek answered. "I can see your lovely face and all its delightful nuances and expressions quite clearly. Experiencing true darkness for we Draknos is rare."

"The perfect predator."

"I suppose. Only these days, my people don't hunt much of anything, and thank the Sacred Fires for that. Before the *Ansi* banished us here, we had just barely resolved a civil war that had dragged on for centuries."

Amber was startled. "What do you mean 'the *Ansi*

banished you here'? I thought it had something to do with thinning dimensions or something like that!"

Raphek kissed her nose. "I think that's a tale best told another time and somewhere more comfortable. That piece of Terran scum has stopped and exited his vehicle far on the opposite end of town. It sounds as though he has entered a dwelling. I can hear the tap of his shoes on hardwood and the rustle of fabric as though he were removing clothing. Perhaps he's given up after all."

"I really can't decide if you're just pulling my chain about being able to know what someone is doing miles away by sound and smell alone," Amber said, shaking her head.

She could barely make out Raphek's frown in the gloom. "Pulling your chain?"

"Teasing."

"Ah. I suppose time and a copious amount of demonstrations will answer that one for you."

She hugged Raphek more tightly. "Just not out here."

"Yes. It's time I return Matty's mother back to him."

Amber pressed her forehead against his chest and closed her eyes for a brief moment as an abrupt maelstrom of emotions washed through her and nearly made her legs give out. It was a close call with the Creepy Mechanic Guy, but she had actually managed to complete her objective relatively unscathed. She might have a new set of finger-shaped bruises on the arm that local asshole had grabbed, but considering how close she had come to really being killed only just yesterday, that a few small bruises were her only injuries tonight was definitely a win.

She definitely hadn't had many of those lately.

"Let's go, and on the way, you can explain what or who the *Ansi* are."

CHAPTER FIFTEEN

Amber half-expected to be greeted at Emma's door by Matty making a mad dash into her arms followed by Jaws of the Grin of Nightmares. Instead, it was the Terran woman, herself, who filled the doorway, alone, and beckoned them inside with a finger to her lips.

"He's been asleep the whole time," Emma informed her softly as they followed her deeper into the room towards the seating in the back.

Their pet mog was nowhere to be seen. Maybe, like a lot of dogs, Jaws slept inside a pen at night.

"Not surprising. The little one's had quite the day," Raphek said.

Amber was immensely relieved. During both the flight to Oklahoma and back, she had fretted about

Matty's reaction to waking up with her nowhere to be found while his mother was off running around in the dark a whole state away and kissing dragon-men.

Matty was still in the same spot on the couch Raphek had lain him across, curled up on his side and hugging his T-rex plushie tightly. Emma's mate, Sevek, was seated next to his feet, the same tablet in his hands as he had used yesterday. It looked as though he had been watching a movie.

"Did you manage to contact the Houston authorities?" Sevek asked just as softly.

"Yes, though I'm not sure if they one hundred percent believed it was me," Amber replied with a weary sigh, "but no doubt they've already traced the cell phone signal to whatever cell tower services Kingston. They'll find out it was really me soon enough. They had me talk to an FBI agent."

Emma winced. "Having the FBI involved always complicates things."

"That's why I ended the call when he started trying to coax me to go back to Houston. I told him about all of Garrett's past abuse and that I was in the process of filing for divorce as well as an Order of Protection. I hung up before he could comment."

Emma and Sevek exchanged a look. "Do you actually have a lawyer?"

"I do. She's a divorce lawyer that has a practice in Austin. One of my old college friends had an aunt who used her. The aunt's case involved a big, messy custody battle that the aunt eventually won. She's already drawn up the divorce papers and is just waiting for me to give her the go ahead to serve them to Garrett. She thinks I'm trying to get into a women's shelter right now, so that's why I wanted to delay sending them."

Amber's shoulders slumped. "I suppose I'll have to leave the kingdom again sometime in the next day or two to call her for that go ahead."

Another shared look between the couple and then Emma sent the same meaningful look to Raphek.

Raphek stared at Emma for a long moment without any expression before he blinked and said, "I'll need His Majesty's permission, of course, but that's not a bad thought."

"What isn't?" Amber asked warily. Could these dragons also read minds or something? God, she really hoped not!

"A possible opportunity for you," he hedged. "I know you're pretty exhausted, but would you mind terribly waiting here just a bit longer while I go consult with the king briefly?"

"As long as Emma and Sevek don't mind..." Amber said slowly, looking at both Emma and Raphek questioningly, though the wordless question aimed at Raphek was completely different and filled with quite a bit sudden anxiety.

Emma waved off her concern. "No classes to teach tomorrow, remember? I'll have all day tomorrow to nap to my heart's content."

Raphek suddenly leaned down and planted a soft kiss on her mouth before Amber could even react. "We'll take Matty back to my home once I return. As I'm sure the king will be agreeable to what I am about to propose, we can discuss the finer points then."

Amber could only nod. She wouldn't have been able to form a coherent word in that moment if her life depended on it.

"Did I miss something?" Emma asked slyly once the front door had closed behind Raphek.

Amber carefully sat down on the couch on the cushion next to Matty's head. "Yes, but I think I missed it, too."

"Dragons aren't much for beating around the bush," Emma said sympathetically as she settled onto the couch next to her husband. She then turned and gave Sevek a wink. "I prefer that kind of straightforwardness, myself. It saves everyone a lot of grief in the long run. Although —I do believe Raphek was consciously declaring something with that PDA."

"He was," Sevek agreed, his tone a bit startled. "Especially if that was the first time he kissed you."

Amber's hands suddenly became very fascinating. "He—kissed me earlier in Oklahoma when we were waiting for it to be safe for him to shift and launch into the air," she admitted.

Sevek barked a laugh and then winced, looking down at a still-sleeping Matty. Her son didn't even twitch.

"And here I thought he was being rather old-fashioned by announcing his intentions to court you with that kiss just now," Sevek said in a much quieter voice. "I should've known better." When she flashed him a confused look, he elaborated, "Raphek has always been a follow-the-flow-of-a-river kind of male. The kind of rules of etiquette of the ancient royal court that would have once required him, a member of the royal House of the Red Flame, to announce his intentions to court with a chaste kiss before witnesses don't suit his personality at all. You were probably sending him signals that you would be receptive to a courtship by him all day. No need for an announcement first, just mutual attraction. The kiss a few minutes ago was just him casually telling us, his friends, that he was courting you."

"Worse than bloodhounds, like I said," Emma chimed in, shaking her head.

For a split-second, Amber had the urge to cover her face in sheer mortification. Instead, she just let out a quiet chuckle at the absurdity of the whole thing. So what if Emma's husband knew that she had been lusting after Raphek all day, and probably because he had smelled her arousal, himself? She was a grown woman with needs, dammit! It was nothing to be ashamed about at all.

It wasn't.

"I didn't expect that kiss at all," she said, once again looking down at her hands, "but when it did…" Amber trailed off and shrugged uncomfortably.

"Draknos are too damned charismatic for their own good," Emma commiserated. "After all the stuff both Briana and another have told me about their own courtship periods, I'm really starting to believe they're like catnip to us—to us Terran women, I mean."

"I *am* still present in the room," Sevek retorted dryly.

Emma leaned her head onto his shoulder. "Doesn't make that statement any less true, darling," she said affectionately.

So, it's not just because I'm hopelessly weak to affection?

Amber suddenly didn't know how to feel about everything anymore. While she had enjoyed the kiss, that didn't mean that she hadn't felt extremely guilty about taking that short moment for herself. She wasn't even divorced yet, for God's sake! It didn't matter that her marriage wasn't legally recognized in Elysia South or that she had already signed her copy of the divorce papers. That was just semantics. Never mind her relationship status, was it really okay to start a relationship with a man she barely had known for a couple of *days*? Neither Emma nor Sevek seemed to find the thought of them as a couple weird or even scandalous, but…

She looked down at Matty. First and foremost, she had to think of her son, what was best for *him*.

But what if Raphek could be the kind of loving father that Matty's never had?

The second that thought entered her brain, Amber could have slapped herself—hard and several times. Talk about counting your chickens before they hatched. Maybe Raphek's lips had broken something vital in her brain for real—like her common sense.

"Any chatter on social media happen while we were outside the kingdom I should know about?" Amber asked Emma, wanting to change the subject, but at the same time, worried that Creepy Mechanic Guy might stir the pot in a bad way. A loose end like him was always worrisome.

"Just the usual speculation when someone high profile goes missing, especially if that person is tied to a politician," Emma replied. "A lot of people *really* despise

Senator Johnson, so most of the really nasty comments are targeted at him."

"Anything about a reward?"

Sevek snorted. "It was all over the senator's social media. Fifty thousand to the one whose tip brings you and Matty home."

Amber's jaw dropped. "Fifty-k! No wonder that man at the convenience store grabbed me!"

Emma sat up. "Someone *grabbed* you?"

"Yeah, but I kicked him in the balls and was able to run away. Once I got to where Raphek was hiding, he made sure the asshole never found us."

Emma huffed. "Not the most ideal way to spread gossip about you in that town, but I don't doubt for a second that he didn't call the tip hotline."

Amber made a face. "He snuck up on me when I was leaving the store, so he could've taken a picture of me at any time while I was inside the store."

"If so, then no doubt that picture will have been shared online at least a million times a mere hour after dawn," Sevek added. He turned on the tablet that was resting on his right thigh. "Now I'm curious."

Emma pointed at one of the end tables across the room next to their second couch. "If you want to surf, too, while we wait for Raphek to come back, then you can borrow my tablet."

"Thanks."

Amber wasn't particularly in a hurry to run across all the posts that undoubtably said horrible things about her, but even running into those potential gut-wrenching landmines was preferable to allowing her thoughts to stew without the distraction of conversation and make her emotions regarding Raphek even more of a tangled mess than they already were.

Exhaustion suddenly settled onto her shoulders as heavily as thousand-pound weights. What she really wanted to do was sleep, but that was likely a relief she wouldn't experience for many hours, yet.

Seeing Emma and Sevek cuddled so cutely together on the couch while they shared Sevek's tablet made Amber's heart clench painfully. That kind of love was what she had envisioned for her own life when she had accepted Garrett's marriage proposal. The dream had quickly fallen apart within days of saying "I do." Knowing what she knew now, she wondered if the bastard had only asked her to marry him because his father had forced him to in order to protect his reputation for the sake of his political future.

Still, seeing Emma and Sevek also reminded her that such loving relationships happened all the time. Her parents were a good example. Her friend, Keri, was currently engaged to a great guy. Amber had been living under a dark cloud of fear, misery, and anger for so long it was no wonder that she had forgotten that loving relationships were *normal*, not the exception.

Could she have the same with a dragon-man that had showed both her and Matty only kindness? Especially when Matty had already taken such a liking to him. Images of her son tugging Raphek around the Elysian marketplace like a kite flashed through her mind, making her smile.

Amber reached over and carefully, tenderly smoothed away a stray lock of hair off Matty's forehead.

It had been too dark to see Raphek's face after that amazing kiss as he had looked down at her. She found she really wanted a chance to see what emotions his eyes had held after such a passionate moment.

However, before that, she and Raphek needed to have a serious talk.

Sleep could wait.

CHAPTER SIXTEEN

Luckily for Amber's peace of mind, Raphek returned after being gone for only a little over an hour. Once she had made up her mind that she did indeed want to pursue a relationship with Raphek, time had seemed to crawl until she had been ready to start pulling her hair out in frustration. The fact that her eyes had kept straying to the tiny time display at the top of Emma's tablet every few seconds or so hadn't helped matters one bit.

That Raphek immediately claimed the spot on the couch next to her made her immensely happy and yet, at the same time, quite irritated with herself that such a mundane action could cause such a strong reaction in her. Even so, for a split-second, Amber contemplated reaching for his hand and threading their fingers together in a sudden mad desire to feel his warmth, to prove to herself that the intimacy his actions seemed to be offering her was real.

She didn't move a muscle.

"I swear, Raphek, you have one of the best poker faces I've ever seen," Emma complained. "Good news, bad news, you always look like you just spent a couple of hours in your meditation room."

He shrugged. "I've never been the excitable type."

"Given that your conference with the king was fairly short, I would guess that things went well," Sevek noted.

Amber's impatience didn't think over an hour was fairly short, but to someone like Raphek that had lived for thousands of years, they likely didn't have an impatient bone in their body. Was Sevek as old?

Raphek nodded, his lips curving up slightly and lightening the intense expression in his eyes. "Given recent events, His Majesty agrees that both Airon and your sister may greatly help move along our objectives. He wants us to set up as many legal protections in the Terran world for Amber as possible. Thus, he's given me permission to contact Airon in Dallas."

"Sister?" Amber asked, looking between Raphek and her hosts questioningly.

"Mine," Emma answered. "Her name is Lillian. She's

a lawyer that's mated to Raphek's best friend, Airon. They live in Dallas."

"They live in—wait, wait!" She turned incredulous eyes to Raphek. "Since Airon's *your* best friend, does that mean he's a *dragon*? A dragon living *outside* Elysia South?"

"He is," Raphek said as calmly as if he were commenting on a sunny day and not confirming something so utterly important and dangerous.

"My parents, Lily's best friend, and one set of her neighbors—long story—are the only Terrans that know Airon's a Firedrake," Emma said. "Although no one in Washington is aware, Lily has been acting as King Dagon's lawyer ever since I married Sevek."

"Airon works as one of many of the king's eyes and ears beyond the kingdom," Raphek added.

"You can probably see where this is going," Emma said. "Those two are best equipped to deliver a message from you to your divorce lawyer. Lily has several friends in Austin that probably run in the same legal circles as your lawyer."

"Airon normally comes here to deliver reports to the king once a month," Raphek told her. "He's due for a visit in another two weeks, but I don't think we can wait that long to act. It's important to deal a blow to Garrett's reputation before a damning video of the incident at the border surfaces."

"A paper trail that's easily accessible to the public is always a good thing to have in these sorts of messy situations," Emma agreed.

"That's why I needed His Majesty's permission to contact him," Raphek concluded.

"...because you'll have to leave the kingdom again," Amber said, a feeling of dread washing through her.

Raphek gently touched her shoulder. "I won't have to fly to Dallas to meet him if that's what you're worried about."

Damn. Bloodhound nose. Right. Amber wasn't sure she would ever get used to being such an open book even when none of her true thoughts and feelings showed on her face.

"We have a ton of burner phones we can use," Emma explained.

"We just can't use them anywhere near the kingdom," Raphek added. "One call and Airon, at the very least, will be able to come by midday barring any unforeseen complications. Sneaking Lillian into the kingdom is a bit trickier and usually takes a couple of weeks to set up securely."

"Like you, I had a very good reason to suddenly become incommunicado," Emma said with a self-deprecating grin, "and because of that, Lily's activities are always being scrutinized by the powers that be."

It was only then that all of Emma's cryptic statements about herself finally clicked, and Amber gasped in sudden shock.

"You're that elementary school teacher, aren't you?" Amber blurted, "The one that was caught by the military for trying to get close to the energy barrier only a few days after Elysia South appeared in our world!"

"And court martialed," Emma said with a grimace, "but yeah, that was me. Another *really* long story for another time."

It was no wonder Emma had been so secretive about herself. For Emma to trust her now with so many secrets... A knot formed in Amber's throat. After the mess she had made of everything simply by showing up at that damned dragon-viewing platform on the strength of what turned out to only have been a rumor, treating her as though they now considered her and Matty one of *them* versus the rest of humanity...

A pair of arms as hard as steel suddenly wrapped around her, and she found herself being cradled against Raphek's magnificent chest before she could even blink. "I know it's a lot to take in," Raphek murmured into her hair.

Amber was sure her face resembled a cherry. What

was it with dragons and PDAs? Of course, her bashful- ness didn't keep her from relaxing into his embrace. God, but he really was so deliciously warm. She imag- ined she could easily fall asleep within his arms—if she weren't so worried about Raphek leaving again.

"Maybe you should take Amber and Matty back to your place and get them settled for the rest of the night before you head out again, Raphek," Emma suggested. "Remember, Amber needs sleep, doubly so since it wasn't that long ago that Lady Serie healed her."

As if I'd be able to sleep while you're out risking your life for me, Amber thought grimly, but getting their new bedding set up in the room Raphek had given them would give her the chance to be alone with him for a few moments before he left.

Amber reluctantly pulled out of his arms and said, "Yes, we've kept Emma from her own rest long enough. Thanks so much for watching Matty again on such short notice."

"Anytime. Remember, I won't be teaching classes tomorrow—or I suppose today since it's already after midnight—so if you need me to watch Matty when Airon arrives, bring him over. I could even introduce him to a boy that lives nearby that's only about a year older than him."

A lump of emotion rose in her throat again at the

thought of Matty maybe making friends here. Matty had rarely gotten to play with children his own age.

"I'll do that, and thanks again for everything."

Just as before, Raphek gathered Matty into his arms for the trek to his home. Apartment? Lair? That last thought almost made her giggle at how absurd it sounded.

"I'm really surprised that he hasn't woken up even once," Amber said quietly as they made their way down the dim corridors towards the lifts.

"Does he usually have trouble sleeping?"

"Sometimes," she replied, looking at him meaningfully. There were too many possible dragon ears around to say more until they were inside Raphek's place.

He nodded.

All their purchases that Raphek had pawned off onto that guardsman that had waylaid them at the lifts were all stacked neatly off to the side in the foyer. Beside them were also a huge stack of cushions of various sizes and thickness that Raphek had purchased for her to use as bedding as well as a roll of thin, soft fabric that she planned to use as a blanket rather than for clothing as was its intended use. They, too, had been delivered.

Raphek gestured towards the cushions with his chin. "Grab one of those large cushions. We can set it in the room for Matty to lay upon while we set up your bedding to your satisfaction."

Once Matty was comfortable, it took them probably ten minutes tops to lug the rest of the cushions and makeshift blanket to the room and arrange them into something like a circular nest very similar to the one he had in his meditation room. It would be strange to sleep so close to the floor, but the cushions were incredibly soft, and for a place that was virtually a fancy cave, the air was cool but nowhere near uncomfortably so. The fabric would be more than adequate to keep them warm.

As she watched Raphek carefully move Matty and gently lay him down in the center of their new makeshift bed, Amber abruptly asked, "Do you want to court me?"

If she hadn't been so exhausted, she doubted she would have been able to be so blunt.

Raphek sighed as he sat back onto his haunches next to Matty. "No doubt Emma has been giving you an earful while I was speaking to the king."

Amber merely looked back at him expectantly, making no move to join them on the cushions. As he quietly regarded her with eyes almost too intense for her to meet, she tugged nervously at the hem of her blouse, but didn't lower her gaze. She hardly dared blink.

"It's not the best of times to start something of such importance, I admit," Raphek said soberly, "but yes, I very much wish to court you."

Amber smiled nervously even as explosions of joy were going off within her. "I want that, too, but I have to warn you. I don't know the first thing about dragon courtships, or royal etiquette, or very much about Draknos at all."

Raphek carefully moved across the cushions on his knees and then climbed back to his feet once he reached the edge and her. The warmth rising in her cheeks seemed to correlate to the warmth radiating off him as he had neared until Amber once again found herself enveloped within his arms.

"Understanding will come naturally in time. You don't need to worry about any of that right now, though I must admit, I'll enjoy teaching you all the delights a dragon can offer."

This wasn't like back in the near pitch darkness of that Oklahoman thicket. Amber could clearly see the desire in his beautiful fire-colored eyes, the way his slightly-larger-than-a-human's pupils dilated as his gaze lingered on her lips. No one, not Garrett or any of the handful of guys she had dated before him had ever looked at her quite like—as though she were the most desirable woman on the planet.

Her heart rate spiked almost painfully. "Raph..." Amber breathed, suddenly unable to form a more coherent thought other than that one syllable.

Her lips were already sensitive and tingling with anticipation when Raphek lowered his head and took her lips in a fierce kiss that she swore made her toes curl. Raphek was such a calm personality, serious and straightforward, so it was a complete surprise how much passion the dragon-man could express in a single kiss.

All too soon, Raphek pulled away until their lips barely touched. "Sleep well," he murmured, his warm breaths against her kiss-swollen lips making her shudder in excitement, "and when you wake, I'll begin my courtship of you in earnest. The morning light may bring with it more troubles, but that doesn't mean you shouldn't enjoy the times between dealing with those troubles."

Amber clenched his shoulders more tightly. The reminder of the shitshow that was probably just around the corner instantly cleared the fog of desire from her mind. When Raphek was kissing her, it was just so easy to forget the crushing weight of all her problems. That was dangerous, she knew it was, but at the same time, she hadn't felt so invigorated in *years*. Maybe Raphek was right. Maybe it was okay to feel a bit of joy even when surrounded by enemies.

Just the thought of seeing Matty's eyes lighting up with pure happiness completely free from the threat of violence that had hovered around them like a poisonous cloud had pushed her to do the utterly insane thing that had landed them to this point where she had seen that very happiness she had hoped for in his eyes in that Elysian marketplace. It was almost inconceivable, but could she find the same kind of happiness with Raphek?

Her lips firmed resolutely as she looked up into his intense eyes. She damned well would fight tooth and nails to find out.

CHAPTER SEVENTEEN

The moment she saw Raphek standing over her, holding Matty and Matty clinging to his neck wearing a huge grin on his face, Amber thought for sure she was dreaming.

Matty was dressed in a light blue tunic that fastened with ties along the side and matching pants of the same linen-like material as the top. His feet were bare. The outfit was unlike anything he had worn before.

However, his clothing wasn't the main reason for her sense of unreality. It was the picture of domesticity that the two presented, like a father holding his son as comfortably as though he had been doing it for years.

Other than instances where he had paraded Matty around his social and donor circles as pretty much a symbol of his bedroom prowess, Garrett had rarely paid his own son attention. Both she and Matty had been his trophies, props, nothing more.

Amber blinked slowly, but the astonishing scene before her didn't change.

"I thought you might be awakening," Raphek said. "I thought it best to bring the little one back in before you could realize he was no longer sleeping beside you."

She sat up so quickly that the room spun as a wash of dizziness hit her, suddenly wide awake. "What in the world…!"

"Mommy, Mr. Dragon let me play in his pool!" Matty informed her happily.

"Pool?" Amber parroted in confusion.

"Matty woke up about a couple of hours ago and decided to go exploring while you slept," Raphek said. "He found me in the sitting room. I hope you don't mind, but I figured I should prepare him for the day. The pool he mentioned is my bathing pool."

Oh. Right. They had both used such a pool at Emma's to bathe before their lunch date with Princess Briana. Her brain must still be half-asleep.

"He let me eat a big grape again," Matty added.

"A lithla fruit," Raphek interpreted.

It took her a while to remember that it was the

eggplant-looking fruit Raphek had bought for Matty at the marketplace yesterday.

"I'm sorry. I probably overslept," Amber said, suddenly flustered as she slipped off the cushion-bed and struggled to her feet. Since there weren't any windows in the room, she had no idea if it was still morning or past noon.

"Not at all," Raphek said as he reached out with his free hand to steady her by the shoulder. "It's only midmorning."

She anxiously ran a hand through her hair, frightfully aware that it probably resembled a bird's nest. "Since you're here, I take it you were able to contact your friend okay?"

"Fortunately, on the first try and without incident. Airon should arrive here within a couple of hours or so."

Matty gestured for Raphek to put him down. He then grabbed Amber's hand and tugged her towards the room's doorless threshold. She still found it weird that none of the rooms had doors, just open portals.

"Come watch cartoons with me and Mr. Dragon," Matty entreated.

That he called Raphek "Mr. Dragon" was just too adorable for words.

"We're going to have company soon. Let Mommy

take a bath and get ready first," Amber replied. She glanced over at Raphek and asked a bit hesitantly, "You don't mind keeping an eye on him for a little bit longer, do you?"

"Of course not," Raphek replied easily.

When Amber emerged from the bathroom a half-hour later, she was once again stunned when she saw Matty snuggled up against Raphek's side as the two sat on the couch watching one of Matty's favorite animated series on Raphek's tablet. The scene made her want to fall to her knees and cry for a week. Only three days earlier, she had despaired of ever finding a place where she and Matty could just *live* without constant fear.

Now, for the first time since she had made that colossal mistake in falling for Garrett's fake charm and accepting his marriage proposal, Amber could see a real future for Matty and her—and it was beautiful.

Rather than comment, she decided to take the bull by the horns and snuggle into Raphek's other side. She nearly melted when Raphek immediately wrapped an arm around her waist and kissed her cheek tenderly.

"Tired of cartoons yet?" Amber murmured.

"This is my first exposure to them," Raphek said. "Minus all the shenanigans, they seem to be lessons of a sort."

Amber laughed. " 'Shenanigans'—where did you even learn that word?"

"Probably the princess. When she first arrived with Prince Astaron in Elysia proper, the prince insisted that everyone in the Royal Guard should learn English. Initially, English was only spoken for clandestine messages between the royals and the Guard."

"Does this have something to do with that civil war you mentioned last night?"

He nodded. "After all the betrayals that ignited that long and devastating war, trust was no longer easily given to those that were not Rekkan. It was only in the last five years before we were banished here that the majority of our people outside of the Guard began learning English out of curiosity."

"And a good thing too considering what country you Firedrakes appeared in," Amber said. "And the other three kingdoms?"

"Once it became apparent that there was no returning home, we sent some of our people to Colorado, Canada, and England as translators and teachers. While the House of the Red Flame has always ruled both the Rekkan and the Ishkkan, the Mikkan and the Sakkan have always had their own rulers."

And the humans have no clue. How many times had

she, herself, looked up into the night sky and not known that a dragon had passed overhead?

"You said the '*Ansi*' did this to you. 'Banished' you here," she said. "Were they another faction of dragons? I've seen someone perform real magic here. Is that how they did it? With some kind of high-level spell?"

Raphek's eyes darkened. "No, not dragons. They aren't shifters at all. The English word that Briana uses for the *Ansi* is 'witch.' "

Amber's eyes widened. "You're kidding me! *Witches?* This is the first I've ever heard of witches being mentioned when people talk about the Draknos!"

"For very good reason," Raphek said gravely. "Some of their ancestors were exiled to this world centuries ago, and though their blood has thinned considerably through the generations as they mated with Terrans, those descendants are still very much able to use the same powerful magical artifact we believe the *Ansi* used to permanently exile us here, as well. We don't want to invite the scrutiny of anyone with *Ansi* blood at all costs."

"I don't blame you," Amber said quietly. Once again, guilt of all the likely trouble she had just brought Raphek's people reared its ugly head. "Hearing all that, I don't understand why you would—"

A loud knock on the double doors that opened out onto the balcony made Amber nearly jump out of her skin. One of the doors opened just as Raphek sighed, but he made no move to disentangle himself from her and Matty.

"Well, well, don't y'all look cozy," a gorgeous, dark-haired man said as he walked inside, his lips stretched in a roguish smirk.

He was dressed in the same kind of robe-like garment Raphek had donned when they had first arrived on Emma's balcony—was it only three days ago? God, it felt like ages ago.

"I expected you to come through the front door, you know, not scare my guests," Raphek retorted dryly.

The man snorted. "Right. *Guests.*"

He then walked over to Amber and held out his hand. "I'm Airon of the House of Embers. It's a pleasure to meet you."

Amber accepted his hand tentatively for a firm shake. "Amber Davis, and that's my son, Matty."

Airon squatted down and smiled gently at Matty who was peering shyly at this newest dragon-shifter even as he clutched at Raphek's arm. "Hey there, little one. I'm happy to meet you, too."

"Hello," Matty said bashfully.

"You made it a bit earlier than I was expecting," Raphek said as Airon moved over to one of the over-stuffed chairs adjacent to her end of the couch. He handed Matty the tablet. "Here, Matty, you can keep watching cartoons while your mother and I talk with Airon."

Airon's cheerful demeanor suddenly melted into something more alert and serious. "I left not long after we hung up, after I filled Lily in on all the important bits, of course. You know that Senator Johnson and his anti-dragon colleagues have been on her radar ever since he introduced that first piece of legislation a couple of years ago to build a permeant military base outside of North Point."

"You said Lillian's secretly King Dagon's lawyer," Amber cut in. At Raphek's nod, she turned her attention back to Airon. "I remember that bill failed to pass in the Senate. Did she help defeat it somehow?"

Airon grinned. "She works with several pro-dragon lobbying groups, so that would be a big yes. However, ever since Senator Johnson's press conference in Houston, she's been on edge. Her contacts in Washington had heard rumors that he had scheduled an emergency meeting with the president for this morning even before yesterday's pressor. That his son's wife and grandson go missing on the eve of such a meeting seemed awfully suspicious, a wife that had been secretly planning a divorce, as it turns out."

Airon winked at her, making her flush.

"After I passed on all the information you gave me," he continued, "Lily's now convinced footage of you reaching your big claw through the shield to snatch up Amber and Matty does indeed exist and that Johnson plans on revealing it to the president in that 'emergency' meeting today."

Raphek muttered a harsh-sounding word that Amber would have bet was a Draknar curse. "So much for our hopes of landing the first blow."

"Not necessarily," Airon countered. "Johnson may show the president the video today, but that doesn't mean she will agree to its release right away or even at all. At the very least, she will want to speak to His Majesty first before deciding to do anything."

"Henry will just release the video anyway even—no —*especially* if President Mitchell forbids it," Amber warned. "He'll just pretend to be shocked and claim that it must have been leaked by one of the people at the dragon-viewing platform."

"He *is* the type," Airon conceded, "but even so, I don't think the leak will happen today or even tomorrow. His Majesty can stall President Mitchell for a few days by first, pretending to be affronted by the accusation and then claiming he will investigate the matter on our end."

"If footage does indeed exist and an edited version is shown to President Mitchell, then the king is already prepared to admit that some aspects of the video are true but does not, of course, tell the true story," Raphek said. "He will also claim that we rendered medical aid to Amber and then she left the kingdom with her son the next day of her own volition. I didn't tell you this when we spoke earlier, but I flew Amber to a small town in Oklahoma last night before I called you so that she could call the Houston authorities and provide physical proof that she was not within Elysia South any longer."

"Smart," Airon said with an approving nod. "That you have already begun seeding the Terran lands with Amber's footprints, so to speak, just might make what I'm about to propose work even better."

"You want me to be seen somewhere else in the country," Amber guessed, a huge surge of trepidation instantly rising in her gut. She felt Raphek stiffen beside her.

Airon nodded. "And not just anywhere." His eyes fixed apologetically on Raphek. "I know we talked about me flying a message signed by Amber tonight to her divorce attorney in Austin, but I think we can, as the

Terrans say, kill two birds with one stone if I take Amber along with me and she makes a surprise, in-person visit in the morning, instead. Even better, Otaron has established a Draknos safehouse just outside the city limits, so there will be virtually no risk of her being seen in the area prematurely. Otaron can also help us with things such as securing rideshares and burner phones for Amber when she must navigate Austin alone."

"If Amber agrees and His Majesty agrees, then *I* will fly her down myself," Raphek said, intense eyes practically daring his friend to argue.

Airon held his hands up in surrender. "I have no objections if His Majesty doesn't. Two set of eyes is always better than one in these kinds of tricky operations."

"It's a good plan," Amber said reluctantly, her eyes sliding towards Matty, who was so absorbed in the cartoon he was watching that she doubted he had heard a word they had said. If King Dagon okayed the plan, then this would be the first night Matty would have to spend without her nearby since they had entered Elysia South. God, she hated having to leave him, but if she didn't, then the nightmare of her soon-to-be-ex's family's machinations would never end.

Raphek's arm tightened briefly around her waist

before he slowly released her. "Then let's go speak with the king."

"We'll need to stop at Emma's first," Amber said. She reached across Raphek and gave Matty's sleeve a tug to get his attention. "Hey sweetie, do you want to go over to Emma's again today while Mommy and Raphek work? Emma told me she wants to introduce you to a new friend who lives near her."

CHAPTER EIGHTEEN

By the time night had fallen, Amber was so anxious about leaving again that she could barely eat anything. However, she had forced down as much of the dinner Raphek had prepared for both her and Airon as she could, aided by the thought of how stupid it would be to faint in her lawyer's office and screw up everything just because she had been too nervous to eat.

As she stood in the pitch black darkness next to the camouflaged entrance to the firedrakes' secret tunnel waiting for Raphak and Airon to shift to their dragon forms, Amber suddenly had a powerful urge to see Matty one last time before they left for Austin. However, as soon as the thought entered her mind, she knew that it was a bad idea even if it weren't much too late for that given that they were already outside of the kingdom.

She had already explained to Matty when they had dropped him off at Emma's that he would be having a sleepover with Emma, Sevek, and Jaws in addition to meeting the little boy that lived on Emma's level. Matty had taken the information with a measure of excitement, but if he saw her again after he hadn't seen her for most of the day…

Yeah, it was best for *both* of them to wait until she was picking him up to see each other.

If Airon hadn't been present, she would have watched them shift, but though Raphek might not mind her seeing him nude, she *definitely* didn't want to see Raphek's best friend nude, even by accident. She frowned. Not that she would have been able to see much detail in this gloom, anyway.

The mechanics of shifting fascinated her. It happened so fast that Amber had not been able to really tell how exactly a man could grow and change into something so fundamentally different in composition as a dragon.

If her whole mess of a life ever settled down, then the mechanics of shifting would be one of the first of the million plus questions she was dying to ask Raphek about the Draknos.

Amber was startled out of her wistful thoughts when a large, red-scaled dragon head with black horns abruptly filled her entire vision, his eyes glowing an eerie red mixed in with the fire-orange of his irises.

"Ready to go?" the dragon she assumed was Raphek rumbled, his breath hot and smelling of something metallic like ozone rather than the sulfur she had half-expected.

"I'm ready for this to be over and done, yes," she replied with a forced smile as she reached out a hand to briefly touch the side of his snout.

Just as the scales on his hands had been, the scales of his face were warm. The thought that she was petting a *dragon* almost made her giggle, but she swallowed it down. This was neither the time nor the place for giggling.

Raphek closed his eyes and made a brief sound of pleasure before he lifted his head away from her. Amber stepped away from the tunnel entrance and looked over at Airon. At first glance, his dragon form appeared identical to Raphek's, but she was sure if she had the time to compare them, the pattern of scales all over their bodies as well as the tint of black in their wings would be completely different.

At any rate, they were the most magnificent beings she had ever seen.

Raphek held out a hand, palm up, and after tossing the large, cloth drawstring bag with their changes of clothes onto it, Amber climbed on.

"Next stop on Dragon Airlines is Austin, Texas," Airon quipped with a grin full of teeth that made her reptilian brain shudder.

"Let's just hope there won't be any turbulence," Amber muttered as Raphek made a dome over her with his other hand.

Amber didn't speak again until after they had been flying for about five minutes. "To tell you the truth, I didn't think we would be doing this at all, tonight."

"You thought His Majesty wouldn't agree to our plan?" Raphek asked.

She didn't think she would ever get used to how she could feel the vibrations of his voice wash over her whenever he spoke in this form.

"That's not it. I honestly thought a video of us would have dropped long before nightfall. Yet, the president didn't even call King Dagon like we thought. This whole lotta nothing from the senator makes me really nervous."

"As it does me," Raphek admitted. "Even so, giving yourself a second footprint, as Airon calls it, in Austin remains our best move right now. Airon and I will watch all the social media and news sites all night while you sleep to make sure nothing significant happens before dawn."

Amber rested her check against one of Raphek's enormous talons and closed her eyes wearily. "I pray that nothing does."

She was just so damned exhausted, body and soul. She wanted this whole mess *over*.

The sound of two pairs of wings flapping in the wind was hypnotic, so much so that Amber didn't realize that she had dozed off until she felt her stomach lurch unpleasantly as Raphek began to descend.

"I didn't mean to fall asleep," Amber said as she rubbed the remaining sleep out of her eyes. Dammit, now she would have a harder time falling asleep for the rest of the night.

"You haven't been getting enough, so I'm not surprised," Raphek replied. "We'll be at the safehouse in a few minutes. You'll be able to sleep again after we've spoken to Otaron."

"I'll be fine," she insisted.

Once they landed, Amber spent a few seconds purposefully yawning to try to make her ears pop before Raphek removed his hand. The first thing she noticed were all the dark silhouettes of trees only a few feet before her, as though they were at the edge of a woodland. A quick glance to the right and left showed more clusters of trees. She could also hear the faint sound of running water. Was that the Colorado River?

Bag in hand, Amber stiffly slipped off Raphek's palm and indulged briefly in a good stretch. She turned around in enough time to see Raphek begin his shift. Although she knew she shouldn't, Amber watched keenly as his body seemingly compressed down like a strange morphing effect into the form she was most familiar. Even in the gloom, she could see that he was not only well-muscled everywhere, but also very, *very* well-endowed.

She had already caressed those muscles with her hands over his clothes the last time they had kissed. She wondered what it would be like to trace those hills and valleys with her tongue, or…

Before her cheeks could go nuclear, Amber busied herself with opening the bag to retrieve his clothes. She found she couldn't look him in the eye as she handed him the clothes and made a big show of turning away as he dressed, wondering if he had caught her ogling him. She was immensely glad that Airon had carried his own change of clothes in that moment.

"You made good time," an unfamiliar voice suddenly

said behind them, pretty much scaring the shit out of her.

Amber whirled around and saw a dark-haired man with the same amount of stubble as Airon standing next to a now fully-dressed Raphek.

"The currents were reasonably stable tonight," Airon said as he stepped up to the two men. "It's good to see you, Otaron. The scents of Austin drive you crazy yet?"

Otaron made a face. "Nearly. The exhaust output per minute is enough to make me swear off Terran cities for eternity."

Raphek beckoned for Amber to join him, and she hurried to his side, still unable to calm her racing heart. "Amber, this is Otaron of the House of Scattered Cinders. He'll be our host for the next day or so."

Otaron nodded politely. "It's nice to meet you, Amber." He then grinned sheepishly. "Sorry about the abrupt entrance."

Amber winced internally. Her heartbeat probably sounded like a million thundering hooves to dragon ears.

"It's nice to meet you, too."

At least her voice didn't shake.

"I've been keeping an eye on all the online chatter while you were in the air, but so far, I didn't see anything that would change our plans for tomorrow,"

Otaron said as they followed him inside a large two-story ranch house that suddenly made Amber wonder where in the world the dragons had gotten the money to afford a property like this. The real estate prices in Austin were some of the highest in the state.

The inside décor was one hundred percent Terran. The living room where they were all now currently seated looked like something from an interior designer's portfolio. Anyone who saw it would never equate it with dragons, and that was probably the point. The house didn't look lived in at all. Everything from the throw pillows to the curtains looked way too pristine. She had made the assumption that Otaron lived there, but now she was sure she was wrong.

"And the lawyer's office?" Raphek asked.

Otaron shook his head. "I sat 'working' pretty much all day at the coffee shop across from Ms. Madden's law practice and didn't see anything out of the ordinary. Lots of suits, of course, but no familiar faces related either to the senator or any of the anti-dragon groups I'm currently aware of."

Amber stared at Otaron in astonishment. "If I didn't know better, and if you didn't have the eye color you have, I never would've even suspected that you were a dragon-shifter. Aside from the barely noticeable accent, you speak like you were born and raised in America."

"I'm thrilled to hear you think so," Otaron said with a pleased smile. He pointed at his eyes. "I hide these with brown-tinted contacts whenever I'm among Terrans. The accent, I'm afraid, is still very much so a work in progress, much to my chagrin."

She nodded. That fact was something she already knew as Airon would be loaning Raphek a pair of his own colored contacts to use while Raphek and Airon shadowed her tomorrow.

"What's the status on transportation?" Airon asked.

"After we drop Amber off at that twenty-four-hour diner at the edge of the city I told you about, a college buddy of mine will send a rideshare over to pick her up. We'll use the old car trouble excuse if anyone asks."

"College?" Amber echoed incredulously. "You've already managed to go to college?"

"Still going," Otaron corrected. "Being a student is a fantastic way to gather information. There's always somebody blabbing something important without me having to say a word. Most of the time, all I need to do is sit anywhere on campus with a book in my lap and listen. I'm known as Oliver Redmayne here. Ollie for short." He bared his teeth playfully at Airon. "Not all of us have a name that sounds identical to a Terran name. I've nearly slipped and given someone my real name more than once."

Airon laughed. "I still have to deal with all the 'You sound funny. Where are you from?' questions, so my name's not that much of an advantage. Your accent is enviously less noticeable than mine. I've pretty much got a handle on all the various idioms and current slang the Terrans in this country use along with those in the UK for good measure. I would wish that a few thousand years of specific vocalizations were as easy to alter as languages."

"Hopefully, I won't find the need to speak at all with any Terrans," Raphek said. "I'm woefully less practiced in speaking English than you two."

"Don't jinx it," Amber scolded half-seriously. "I'm already worried that Ms. Madden will be too booked with clients to see me right away. I shudder to think that I might have to wait in her practice's lobby for hours, out in the open where everyone can see. Take pictures. Make phone calls…"

"I'll loan you a pair of sunglasses just in case," Otaron said. "Unless someone is specifically looking for you there, you'll just look like a thousand other young blonde women in the city at a glance. These days, most people don't look up from their phones long enough to even look at each other, anyway."

"Only my friend, Keri, knows that Taylor Madden is my lawyer and only because she was the one that introduced us," Amber said. "I didn't even tell my parents about her or even that I planned to ask Elysia South for asylum. No one knew about that last bit."

"And we'll keep it that way," Raphek said firmly, taking her hand into his and giving it a reassuring squeeze.

Amber expected at least Airon to comment on them holding hands—he had been teasing Raphek about their budding relationship all day—but he didn't even so much as smirk in their direction.

Instead, it was Otaron who raised an eyebrow. "You're courting then?" he asked Raphek.

Raphek nodded.

"I wondered," Otaron said with a smile.

It was then that Amber remembered their bloodhound noses, and realized with horror that her scent had likely been saturated with her arousal when her mind had been in the gutter after seeing Raphek naked—and that Otaron had been there, too.

Seriously, how in the world was privacy possible among the Draknos?

It took every ounce of her willpower to keep from blushing. She wasn't altogether sure she had succeeded, and that was somehow worse.

"You two should take the rest of the night for yourselves," Otaron continued. "We've done all we can to prepare for tomorrow. I can't imagine with everything that's been happening that Raphek's been able to court you much at all."

"Otaron and I are more than enough to keep an eye on the news and social media until morning," Airon seconded. "Take Amber upstairs. A couple of the rooms should be fully furnished bedrooms. A little alone time will be good for both of you."

Apparently, privacy *wasn't* a word the Draknos knew at all.

Still—it wasn't as if their suggestion didn't have merit…

Amber jumped to her feet. "Come on," she said, pulling once on their joined hands to urge Raphek to stand. "You can show me where I can sleep tonight."

Let all the dragons make of that what they will—including Raphek.

Anticipation welled up within her. Amber wasn't altogether sure what she wanted to happen tonight, but she hoped to God that "anticipation" wasn't something a dragon could smell. She didn't want Raphek's actions once they were alone to be colored by her wants. She wanted to know that the desire she had seen in his eyes had been real and not something she had seen because she wanted it so desperately to be true.

Because Airon was right. She needed a bit of "me

time" to keep her mind off the billion and one things that could go wrong tomorrow once she stepped foot into Austin. Worrying herself sick all night wouldn't do anyone any favors. So why did she still feel guilty as Raphek led her up the stairs?

CHAPTER NINETEEN

"So, that was subtle," Amber muttered as she sat gingerly on the corner of a photo-ready king-sized bed filled with artfully arranged decorative pillows. The bed didn't even take up half of the large bedroom. It was likely the master as it had an en suite bathroom.

She watched as Raphek strode across the room to deposit the cloth bag with their change of clothes onto the wide dresser, suddenly feeling unbearably nervous. She had half-expected Raphek to push her up against the nearest wall the moment they had stepped foot into the room, to begin devouring her. That would have been easy, mindless yet exciting, but when had her life ever allowed her to take the easy path?

"We dragons aren't much for subtlety," Raphek said apologetically as he leaned against the dresser.

She chuckled nervously. "I'm starting to realize that." After a few seconds of indecision, Amber kicked her shoes off and then scooted farther onto the bed.

Raphek followed her movements keenly, his eyes unblinking and intense. "I should let you rest."

A sense of utter disappointment instantly inundated her, and it was all Amber could do to keep it from showing on her face. "Stay" was on the tip of her tongue, but the word that actually emerged was a quiet, "Okay."

Not wanting to see him leave, Amber turned and started to toss a few pillows off the bed. She felt a pang of guilt about treating someone else's property with so little regard, but her desire to hide under the covers before Raphek could see her face crumple was stronger.

The sound of Raphek's footsteps on the hardwood made Amber's heart clench painfully, but she didn't look up from her task. She pulled back the comforter as calmly and casually as her—dammit—shaking hand could manage. That was why she nearly swallowed her tongue when a scorching hot arm abruptly wrapped around the middle of her back, and the freaking sun drew in towards her neck.

"Allow me to keep you warm instead as you sleep," Raphek murmured against her right ear, and Amber swore her heart literally skipped a beat at what was quite possibly the sexist bedroom voice she had ever heard.

"O-okay."

And that didn't sound lame at all…

A gentle kiss to the side of her neck followed, making Amber shiver and the hairs at the nape of her neck rise.

Amber was practically putty in his hands as Raphek drew her down prone onto the mattress until they were spooning, his right arm slipping around her middle just under her breasts. Being enveloped by so much warmth and the hardness of seemingly acres of delicious muscles was incredible, and they weren't even skin-to-skin yet! It was laughable that he expected her to fall asleep with such a dragon god in her bed. She had never been more awake in her life!

Or maybe…

"Touch me. Please…" Her voice was barely more than a breath.

Raphek's arms briefly tightened around her and then his lips replaced the warm exhales against her neck. This time, the kiss was firmer with a bit of suction, teasing. Amber let out a sharp breath as the suction continued along her neck. She pressed the length of her body back more firmly against his front, her ass rubbing once against his jeans-covered cock. He answered with a rough thrust of his hips, followed by the sensual glide of a silky tongue tracing the trail he had just kissed up her neck.

Amber gasped again when she felt one of his hands slip beneath her shirt and slowly slide across her belly then up, teasing across the hem of her bra. She grabbed his forearm and pushed it higher in wordless encouragement. His fingers slipped beneath the hem, and with a firm upward yank, both breasts were freed from their satiny confinement.

Raphek ran a thumb over her already hardened right nipple, igniting pinpoints of pleasure, before he cupped both breasts and began to aggressively knead them even as he insistently thrust his hardness against her ass and nipped at her neck with sharp teeth. Amber moaned at this sudden onslaught of so many different sensations, an insistent throb beginning to awaken between her legs.

She reached an arm behind his head and gripped a handful of his hair to pull him away from her neck as she turned her face up for a kiss which he immediately gave. The kiss began slow, a gentle sucking of her lips and meeting of tongues sliding lovingly against each other. The feel of his stubble against her cheeks and chin was a new sensation that she found pleasurable and seemed to heighten the kiss.

Amber soon turned within his embrace until she was facing him, and they could more easily deepen the kiss. Within seconds, Raphek was devouring her with the same fierce passion as he had that night in Oklahoma.

His hands moved down Amber's back and possessively cupped her ass as he continued his earlier grind of his hips against her body. Only this time, his hardness rubbed against her throbbing, though equally covered, sex. Her hips matched his rhythm as she wrapped a leg around his side, desperately trying to press them closer together.

Not close enough—she needed—

As though reading her mind, Raphek abruptly rolled them over until she felt the full weight of his body press her deep into the mattress for the space of one glorious gasp. Then he broke the kiss with a gasp of his own that she found incredibly sexy.

"I want to taste your skin," he growled against her lips, making Amber both shudder and throb harder between her legs.

"God yes."

Raphek gave her another deep kiss that stole her remaining breath and then pulled away and up onto his knees, straddling her body. He pulled his T-shirt over his head and tossed it onto the floor. Amber watched almost in a daze while he unbuttoned his jeans and pushed them down his hips, boxers and all. Her eyes widened when his cock sprang free. Had she really thought it large before? Erect, it truly was impressive—and a bit intimidating.

After his jeans and boxers joined his shirt over the side of the bed, he reached down to grasp the hem of her own T-shirt. Amber tore her gaze away from his member and hastily lifted her arms over her head as he removed it. Her jeans were unbuttoned and yanked halfway down her legs before she could even blink.

When only her socks and panties remained, Raphek paused and just seemingly drank her in from head to toe with his eyes. Heat instantly invaded her cheeks, and Amber had the sudden urge to dive under the blankets beneath her. She fisted the comforter tightly. Her mind had been swimming with so much pleasure that she had completely forgotten about the handful of stretchmarks from her pregnancy that stood out quite vividly on her lower belly. She knew that they shouldn't bother her; they were just a natural part of motherhood, but then Garr—

No.

Amber slowly released the comforter that she had been clenching like a lifeline. The doubts, the self-castigation that asshole's words had caused her. That part of her life was over. The final nail would be driven in once she talked to her lawyer tomorrow. She would *not* allow any of those destructive feelings from her old life ruin things for her here with Raphek.

Raphek was still watching her keenly, only now his eyes were less dark with lust and more—wary. Damn. No doubt her scent had betrayed her sudden anxiety.

Amber held out her arms to him. "I'm just a bit shy about my body," she admitted. "That's all."

Raphek leaned down and gave her a sweet kiss on her mouth. "Your body is beautiful," he said, "so soft and flushed with the color of Terran roses."

The intensity of his fire-colored eyes was almost too much to bear as he complimented her. She wanted to look away, but his gaze seemed to catch and draw her in like a moth to a flame. The arousal that had almost dimmed to nothing flared back bright and needy under that heavy gaze.

Slowly, Raphek lowered himself down even farther until their chests were almost touching, propped up with a forearm on either side of her head. Amber reached up and clutched at his shoulders, her breath catching in anticipation.

"Maybe you taste like a rose, too."

Raphek took her lips again, his kiss just as thorough

and passionate as before her little freak-out. When she was breathless and panting again, the silky fire of his lips left her mouth and slowly set a path ablaze down her chin, neck, until they finally stopped to latch onto her right nipple.

"Raph!" Amber moaned as he sucked hard before drawing back to swirl his tongue over the hyper-sensitive bud teasingly.

Amber tangled her fingers in his thick hair and tugged a few times in encouragement. She then arched up with a cry when Raphek unexpectedly pinched her other nipple. He chuckled against her breast, the vibrations sending pleasant shivers throughout her chest. After nipping playfully at the little bud he had been tonguing, he gave the other a final pinch as he resumed his journey down her belly with his mouth. He paused to dip his tongue into her bellybutton a couple of times, making her flinch and gasp as it both tickled and made adrenaline shoot up her spine.

Then as she gazed down at him with heavy-lidded eyes, Raphek began to trace a couple of her more reddish stretchmarks with his tongue. Self-consciousness started to rear its ugly head again but then her panties were suddenly sliding down, and Raphek's tongue licked over a different bud.

...and Amber didn't give a damn about the marks anymore.

Oral sex was something she had never experienced but had always been curious about. That it was happening finally was enough to almost short-circuit her brain. Then Raphek twirled his tongue in some incomprehensible way, and her brain *did* short-circuit as a lightning bolt of pleasure shot up her spine from her sex.

Amber moaned as she fisted the comforter again and mindlessly began to writhe against Raphek's mouth as he slowly melted her brain with the power of his tongue, alone.

"Too much…too…Raph…*please…!*"

A few more garbled, nonsensical words and pleas made it past her lips before her entire body seemed to explode with pleasure, and Amber nearly tore a hole in the comforter as a noise that was half scream, half moan was torn from her throat.

Raphek mercilessly continued to lave attention on her clit until she swore she was about to explode again. Yet, he pulled away before it could happen, making her groan, with need or relief, she wasn't sure.

"You taste even sweeter than the scent of roses," he said as he kissed the inside of one of her trembling thighs.

"Liar," she said through a half-choked laugh.

That had been even better than she had imagined. That she was still so hungry for him after such a mind-blowing orgasm was something equally as astonishing. When Raphek settled between her legs and Amber felt the heat of his cock rub deliciously against her folds, she immediately thrust up against him with a moan and wrapped her legs around his waist.

Raphek grunted and then crushed their lips together at the same time he began to slowly rock his hips, his member caressing her clit with each stroke. When he finally pulled away from her lips, Amber was startled to see that his pupils had shifted to the vertical slits of a dragon's. Uncanny and beautiful, the sight of them made her heart race, not in fear, but something like unbridled excitement, maybe.

"Make love to me," Amber pleaded, pulling him in by the shoulders for another kiss.

Amber's gasp was swallowed greedily by Raphek when his impressive cock abruptly thrust into her passage. Just the head, but it was enough to make the core of her already feel almost stretched to the limit. She dug her nails into his shoulders, likely too deep, but Raphek didn't even twitch as he continued to distract her with tongue and lips while he slowly, carefully continued to press his member forward inch by inch with what had to be the patience of a saint.

Once he was finally fully seated what felt like hours later, for the first minute or so, his cock felt almost too hot. Yet, when Raphek began to slowly pull out just a few inches and thrust back in with a bit of force, the heat became just one facet of the pleasure that was being stoked within her as his strokes sped up and developed a steady rhythm.

Indescribable heat and wet kisses and the feeling of being deeply connected to someone—sex had never before felt like this. She was *seen*; she was being pleasured within an inch of her life, and she knew from the affection and desire she could clearly see even within eyes as alien as a dragon's eyes, his intense focus on her every reaction, that Raphek immensely enjoyed pleasuring her into incoherence.

He had said she was beautiful earlier. Until this moment, seeing reflected through the emotions in his eyes what he saw when he looked at her, Amber hadn't really believed him.

When her second orgasm hit, though it was less intense than her first, her mind was so full to bursting with revelations and emotions she had never felt that tears began spilling down her cheeks even as Amber cried out in utter ecstasy.

The sound of her voice filled with such elation seemed to inject frenzy into Raphek's thrusts and lips until he gave one final, heavy thrust that seemed to reverberate deep into her very marrow, and her passage was filled with a surge of his seed that felt just a degree shy of molten. Normally, such an unexpected, alarming sensation would have had her panicking, but after everything Raphek had done to take care of Matty and her since day one, his unrelenting kindness, Amber couldn't believe that he would do something intentionally to harm her, even to sate his own lust.

Thus, Amber merely tightened her thighs against his sides and continued to accept his kisses as though nothing about his climax had been weird or uncomfortable.

It wasn't until much later as she lay with her head pillowed on his chest and his arms snuggly around her waist that Amber realized she had something much more frightening to worry about than getting first-degree burns from a dragon's seed.

She hadn't taken a birth control pill in three days.

CHAPTER TWENTY

Amber never thought the one thing she had been forced to hone from her miserable years married to Garrett that would turn out to be the most useful was her ability to put the most awful things out of her mind and function in public as though everything was rainbows and butterflies. Of course, faking that you were completely fine was a thousand times harder when you're trying to hide the fact that you're freaking out about something potentially life changing from a group of dragons with sensory abilities that might as well be super powers.

At least today, Amber had the perfect excuse to be anxious. As long as dragons couldn't read minds—and so far, none of the dragons she knew had insinuated they could—she could pretend her latest lapse in common sense hadn't happened until she was safely back in Elysia South.

Twenty-three years old and you're still making these kinds of stupid, easily avoidable mistakes, she thought in disgust as she sat at the breakfast nook with Raphek, Airon, and Otaron and tried to at least eat a bit of toast and a strawberry or two.

At least Airon or Otaron hadn't teased them once about last night. She knew damned well that they both had heard every moan from her mouth and rhythmic squeak of the bed. Yet they had greeted them this morning as though she hadn't tried to scream the house down last night. Nor had they commented on the fact that they were currently holding hands under the table.

Draknos were so confusing.

"I recalled something last night while you were sleeping that I meant to ask you before we left the kingdom," Raphek said as he plowed through his second helping of eggs.

"About?" Amber asked, wincing internally at the wariness that crept into her tone.

"When you spoke to that FBI agent over the phone, you told him that you had proof of Garrett's violence towards Matty and you. Was that true or just a bluff?"

Some of her tension melted away. "It's true. I have an audio file of the night that asshole beat both Matty and me bloody that I secretly recorded on my phone right under his nose. It automatically backed up to my cloud account. You can clearly hear Garrett raging and threatening to blacken my other eye while Matty is crying and screaming inconsolably, and I'm crying and screaming that he's bleeding and begging that monster to let me take Matty to the hospital. I, of course, immediately made several copies and stored them on thumb drives in several different places."

"Can they be easily retrieved?"

Amber couldn't help the smug grin that stretched her lips. "Yes. One is back in the room you gave me. I had it in the front pocket of my jeans the day you brought us into Elysia South. It was in a little metal case for protection, so luckily, it didn't get damaged when I took that bad tumble during the gunfight."

"That's great news," Airon said. "It's a powerful piece to play should things go south after today. Senator Johnson has been too quiet since the press conference. It makes my scales itch."

Amber shoved her plate away, her appetite now completely gone. "What time is that rideshare supposed to pick me up at the diner?"

"Two hours from now," Otaron answered. "Don't worry. We still have plenty of time to get there."

"I'm just ready for this whole day to be over."

"As do I," Raphek said, his hand tightening around hers. "I don't like that you'll be in that building alone with me so far away."

"I hear you," Airon said with a grimace that both Raphek and Otaron instantly mirrored.

Amber wondered what that was about, but she sure as hell wasn't about to ask no matter how curious she was. She had a bad history of inadvertently stepping onto other people's landmines. The last thing she needed was to start this day off with such a bad omen.

WHEN RAPHEK PRESSED such a passionate kiss on her before they dropped her off at the edge of the parking lot of the diner, Amber was grateful for that last bit of warmth that only Raphek could give her. It permeated her body from her lips to the tips of her toes like a warm hug from within. With any luck, it would stay with her for hours, yet. She just wished that the kiss hadn't felt as though he were saying goodbye as opposed to *a* goodbye.

She watched Otaron drive off with a huge knot in her throat even though the car only went a few feet to park in one of the slots near the diner's entrance. Amber waited until the three dragon-shifters entered the building before she slipped on the pair of sunglasses Otaron had loaned her and began to walk towards one of the wooden benches out front.

Although this place was a far cry from 6th Street, Amber still felt as exposed as if it were. At least she was the only one outside at the moment, but the diner was still about three-fourths full. Odds were a few people would see her sitting on the bench when they headed out of the building to their vehicles. Hopefully, they would just think she was waiting for a friend and keep on moving.

Amber pulled her burner cell phone from her pocket and then sat on the bench. Heart pounding, for the next ten minutes, she pretended to be reading a book as she waited. Every time she heard the entrance door swing open, a rush of adrenaline would surge through her body. After the third time, it was starting to make her stomach feel queasy.

God, she really hoped Otaron was right about there being no security cameras outside. She probably looked shady as hell with the way she flinched or stiffened whenever someone left the diner or entered.

By the time the red sedan she had been desperately willing to appear finally did, she was nearly a basket case of nerves. She *so* wasn't made for any of this clandestine shit. Before she got into the car, she carefully checked to see if both the license plate and the woman driver matched the descriptions Otaron had given her.

"Good morning. Thanks for coming so far out," Amber said with a smile as she slid into the backseat.

"Good morning," her driver echoed.

After confirming Amber's destination, the woman didn't utter another word for the entire drive into the heart of Austin. Amber was immensely relieved. Some rideshare drivers were way too chatty and nosy for their own good.

Thirty minutes later, they pulled up to a small bank about three blocks from her lawyer's office. Although Amber had never stepped foot in Taylor Madden's practice, she had looked up the building online to make sure she could locate it on sight without having to ask someone for directions.

It took her another ten minutes taking the scenic route down a series of sidewalks past various restaurants, banks, and a hodgepodge of businesses with her eyes seemingly glued to her phone to reach her lawyer's building. Her heart sank when she saw just how many cars were already parked in the small parking lot out front.

"Here goes nothing," Amber muttered under her breath as she pulled open the glass door and entered the lobby.

A surreptitious glance around the room revealed an elderly couple sitting in the far corner talking quietly with each other, a young brunette about her age dressed in a gray business suit sitting a couple of chairs away from the elderly couple with a briefcase on her lap and frowning down at her phone.

A thirty-something blond man dressed in a dark blue business suit was currently talking with the receptionist. A man with silver-streaked auburn hair also dressed in a business suit and holding a black briefcase stood to his left looking completely bored. There was also four other people sitting singly in the room, most staring at their phones or just fidgeting impatiently.

Amber wanted to cry. With this many people already waiting, she was likely to be here for hours just as she had feared.

She approached the receptionist desk just as the two men walked away, hopefully out the door, but she didn't turn to look.

"May I help you?" the receptionist asked, the woman sounding as bored as the silvering man had looked.

"My name is Lucy Stephens," Amber said, giving the alias her lawyer would know her by. "I don't have an appointment today, but Ms. Madden said to come in anyway if there was ever an emergency and she would squeeze me in."

Amber could practically see the skepticism dripping off the woman as she took in Amber's jeans and simple blouse. "Have a seat, Ms. Stephens, and I'll let Ms. Madden know you're here," she instructed tersely.

There was nothing else to do but to smile and murmur a "thank you." Amber selected a seat that wasn't too close to anyone and resigned herself to staring down at a phone screen until probably after lunch. The thought made her regret not trying to eat more at breakfast. She probably should have at least brought a bottle of water with her.

The next two hours were the longest Amber had ever experienced.

The elderly couple, the brunette in the business suit, and Mr. Bored and Mr. Thirty-something all were called back well before Amber. Only a couple of other people had arrived during that two-hour interval, and even one of them was called back before her. It was lucky that she wasn't in a position to see the coffee shop across the street where Raphek and company were observing her and the building because she would have been hard pressed not to keep glancing out the window at it every few minutes.

As far as glancing at *her*, apparently all her worry had been for nothing. No one had even looked at her when she had walked past them to take her seat, and none had looked since. Otaron had been so right about people and their phones.

Unfortunately, all that forced idle time left her mind plenty of time to wander towards her newest possible upheaval. She'd had unprotected sex last night while her birth control schedule had been disrupted. Amber knew that dragon-shifters and human women could have children together since Princess Briana and Prince Astaron had a son. That meant Raphek was well aware, too. What did that mean?

That the possibility of a pregnancy didn't enter his mind just didn't mesh with the type of gravely serious man Raphek had presented from the day she had met him. Still, after spending a few days among the Rekkan, Amber was beginning to understand, not more about them, but just how woefully ignorant about their society and nature she was. It was obvious from the way Airon and Otaron had treated the whole courtship thing and what had happened last night between Raph and her that the old-fashioned human idea of courtships she'd had in mind wasn't the same as a Draknos's courtship. It was entirely possible that having children within Draknos courtships was a common practice.

Amber suddenly had a powerful urge to start bashing her head against the nearest wall. Why hadn't she asked more questions like any normal, sane woman would have?

"Lucy Stephens."

Amber jolted out of her self-castigation. The receptionist was staring at her expectantly. Crap! It was *finally* her turn—and it had to be when she had just finished twisting her emotions into a giant-sized pretzel of anxiety over a possible unplanned pregnancy.

"Ms. Madden says she can see you from now until noon. Not a minute past as she must leave the office to meet another client. Her office is the large one at the end of the hall."

"Thank you."

Yikes. That meant Amber only had twenty minutes to conduct her business.

Her lawyer's brusque voice welcomed her in after one knock. Amber had never met the chestnut-haired forty-something woman sitting behind the desk in person, but she had spoken to her at length three times to date.

"After our last conversation, I have to say that I'm surprised to see you here in person, emergency or not, Mrs. Johnson," Ms. Madden said as Amber took off her sunglasses and sat in one of the empty chairs in front of her desk.

Straight to business. Amber liked that.

"I know that our time is short, so I'll make this as quick as I can," Amber replied. "After the senator's press conference, I thought it would be best to see you and let someone in the professional sphere know that I'm not dead rather than send an email that can't really be one hundred percent proven that it came from me."

"Indeed. The Johnson patriarch acted just as you said he would," Ms. Madden said grimly.

"I know this whole mess is putting you and your practice in an uncomfortable spot, but I appreciate you seeing me today more than you know. Things escalated to absurd levels more quickly than even I expected. Senator Johnson has brought the FBI into my and Matty's so-called missing persons case, and—"

"How do you know this?" Ms. Madden cut in sharply.

"I wanted to end that whole 'missing persons' nonsense, so I called the Houston PD a few hours after the senator's press conference. I was transferred to an FBI agent. I told him about Garrett's abuse and the fact that I was about to serve him with divorce papers but also was going to file a restraining order. I have a legal volunteer at a women's shelter helping me with that last one. The other is why I'm here today."

"You wish to go forward with your divorce proceedings," Ms. Madden guessed, her gaze piercing and a bit uncomfortable. It was no wonder this woman had such a fierce reputation in the courtroom.

Amber took a deep, steadying breath. "I'm finally at a place where I believe I can do so safely for my son, me, and my parents."

"Then you will have to find another attorney to file on your behalf because from this moment on, I no longer represent you."

What?

Amber stared at the other woman's unblinking eyes. "But you said the last time we spoke that you weren't intimidated in the least by Sen—oh no. He got to you, didn't he…" Amber trailed off in rising horror.

She had to get the hell out of there! She—

The door abruptly opened behind her, and Amber jumped so hard that she nearly fell out of her chair.

"Hello, darling. I see you've met my new attorney."

Amber's blood ran cold.

Like a horror movie heroine expecting to see a monster standing behind her, Amber slowly turned around.

…and indeed, a monster there was.

"Garrett."

Amber said his name like an expletive as her ex sauntered into the office like he owned the place. The bastard didn't even bother to shut the door. He reached out a hand as though to touch her hair, and Amber automatically flinched away. She felt sick when an excited, pleased smile stretched across his face like some kind of hideous, open wound.

"I don't have to listen to this," Amber spat out as she jumped to her feet and started to back away. No way was she going to show this asshole her back.

"You'll sit your ass back down if you know what's good for you!" Garrett snarled. "Take another step towards that door before I've had my say, and your dragon friends will wish you were never born! I'll make sure of it personally!"

Amber stilled. "*Dragon* friends? What are you—are you insane?"

Fury instantly flooded Garrett's hazel eyes, darkening and muddying the color to something she knew well and had learned to fear. But—she absolutely couldn't let fear dictate her actions here. Not only Matty, but the Draknos were counting on her not to fuck this up.

"You're the insane one, thinking you can talk to *me* like that, you ungrateful bitch!" he ground out through clenched teeth.

"Fuck. You!" Amber shot back, more than four years of pent up misery and rage suddenly surging up and *needing* to be released. "Matty's not here for you to use against me this time."

"Oh, but he will be," Garrett sneered. "You'll be bringing him to me by six o'clock this evening or else the world will soon see what happened at that dragon-viewing platform a few days ago."

Amber could feel the blood draining from her face so quickly that she suddenly felt lightheaded. "You *are* insane! That dragon saved Matty and I from being gunned down by your father's goons *and you know it!*"

"Do I?" he questioned with a nasty grin. "It's tragic, you see, that my wife was taken and brainwashed by those fucking lizards in Elysia South to see me and the boy's dotting grandfather as the enemy to the point that you would spread such horrible lies about us as well as steal my son away from me in the dead of night."

"That dragon only helped me out of a sense of common decency," Amber said. "I was freaking bleeding out from a gunshot wound in my leg in front of my toddler son, and I guess a 'fucking lizard' didn't think a little boy should ever have to see his mother die right before his eyes as opposed to his own father and grandfather who took out the hit on his mother in the first place. You would really start a war with the Draknos just because one of them wasn't enough of an asshole to let me die?"

Fury flashed in his eyes again. "You're damned right I would! No one takes something that belongs to me without paying a stiff price!"

"You complete *idiot*!" Amber cried. "Haven't you been listening to a word I said! The dragons don't have Matty! After patching up my leg, they sent us on our way! The Draknos may be good Samaritans, but that doesn't mean that they wanted anything more to do with some random human's mess! Is smearing them in the press with your lies just to soothe your ego worth starting World War III: Dragon Edition? Is a mutually assured destruction scenario what you want? Only, all the Draknos kingdoms will be completely safe behind their energy shields that even our bunker busters couldn't scratch while our own cities will be completely susceptible to all the dragon fire being rained down on them from the sky. You *do* realize that before all that happens, the dragons will definitely come for you and your father *first*?"

Garrett stared at Amber for a long, tense moment, his nostrils flaring like an enraged bull's. "You're bluffing."

Amber stared at him in utter incredulity. After having such a plausible nightmare scenario thrown in his face, he was still refusing to even consider it.

She would have to play her ace now. It was the only way.

"I have proof, Garrett," Amber said evenly, catching and holding his gaze.

"Proof?" he echoed suspiciously.

"I have an audio recording of the night you beat both me and Matty. Remember that night, Garrett? It was the night you hit your three-year-old son so hard in the face that his mouth was streaming blood. You can very clearly be heard forbidding me from taking him to the ER. I never thought I would need it because you were egomaniacal and stupid enough to trigger a war with a peaceful people just because you decided to throw a temper tantrum. But it exists, and I *will* release it if you let your father release his video of lies."

Before Amber could blink, Garrett lunged at her and grabbed her around the throat with both hands. "Not if you're dead!" He hissed, squeezing her neck cruelly. The expression on his face was practically demonic.

"Then you'll…never…find Matty!" Amber gasped out as she frantically pulled at his hands, trying not to freak out completely. Ms. Madden hadn't made a peep so far, so Amber doubted she could expect any help at all from the lawyer.

Garrett paused, and the vise around her neck eased

just enough for her to breathe again. "I know where the brat is," he scoffed.

"For the last…time…he's not with…the *damned* dragons!" Amber wheezed. "Even *I* don't know…exactly where he is…right now."

Garrett's eyes narrowed, and he abruptly tightened his hands around her neck again. Amber let out an awful, strangled sound and scrabbled desperately at his hands with her nails. Garrett howled, and suddenly, that terrible, crushing pressure disappeared. Amber gasped after a breath like a drowning woman breaking the water's surface at the last possible second and then promptly lost it again when the back of the bastard's hand struck her hard across a cheek.

Only sheer will kept her on her feet.

Amber instinctually blocked his next blow with a forearm and then shoved him back against Madden's desk with all her strength.

"If you kill me now, not only will you…never find Matty, that audio…file of you assaulting us will be… released online," Amber threatened roughly. "I've left instructions for it…to be released if I don't contact…the people who have it…once a day."

She fell into a coughing and wheezing fit as she slowly backed behind Madden's desk where the woman in question sat frozen with a pinched look on her face.

For one horribly eternal moment, Amber thought Garrett was about to leap over the desk after her, but then he just cursed loudly and growled, "Six o'clock. Emma Long Metropolitan Park. Think you have enough brains to remember that, you dumb bitch?"

When Amber just stared back at him without a word, he muttered one final "bitch" and then turned on his heel to stomp out like a toddler throwing a tantrum.

"How could you sell me out?" Amber rasped angrily into the heavy silence following Garrett's departure. She rubbed at her neck, cringing to think of the bruises that were probably darkening with every painful breath she took. "I guess attorney/client privilege means nothing to you. Neither does people committing attempted murder in your office. You're just another in a long string of lawyers bought by the Johnsons."

"He showed me the video with the dragon," Ms. Madden said tightly.

Amber drew in a sharp breath that nearly set off another coughing fit.

"Even if what you told your husband is one hundred percent true, it won't matter," she said. "The Johnson family is powerful enough to make their version of events the truth. It will look as though I helped my 'obviously brainwashed client' steal a child away from his 'loving' father. Never mind my career, I would be arrested for treason on the spot, for conspiring with the Draknos. By the time Henry Johnson finished with me, his proof would show that I helped the Draknos kidnap numerous women and children as the ringleader of a human-to-dragon trafficking ring. Agreeing to call your husband and stall you long enough for him to fly out here was the only way I could protect myself."

"That dragon didn't have to help me," Amber said quietly, "but he did. Without hesitation despite knowing it could potentially cause a diplomatic incident between our two peoples. His only thought was to save a mother and child from being murdered right before his very eyes."

Then without another word or backward glance, Amber walked out of Taylor Madden's office.

She half expected to run into at least Raphek on the way out. There was no way his super hearing didn't catch that conversation, but the hallway outside Madden's office was empty and quiet. Although she would like nothing more in the world than for Garrett to disappear off the face of the earth, she really hoped that Raphek didn't catch the bastard on the way out.

Murdering a human in cold blood would be the worst thing that could possibly happen after this already godawful day.

However, after what had just happened, Amber knew that she couldn't meet Raphek at the street corner around the block as they had planned. She couldn't allow Senator Johnson to release that doctored video. Despair crashed through her like a cloud of poisonous gas ready to steal the life from her lungs. There was only one way to stop the coming madness she had unwittingly unleashed on the Draknos.

The lobby was conspicuously empty of both the receptionist and clients. Amber's jaw tightened. Likely Ms. Madden had expected shit to hit the fan once Garrett arrived and had instructed one of her employees to clear the building.

Still no dragons. She couldn't believe that Airon and Otaron were still at the coffee shop silently watching. Not after Garrett had almost murdered her so nearby. Had one of them gone after Garrett to possibly learn more about how he planned to carry out his ultimatum to her? They had to have heard the time and meeting place. Was one of them still in the coffeeshop watching to make sure she safely left the building right now?

It would be all over if any of the three followed her now, especially Raph.

Amber put on her sunglasses, took a deep breath, and dashed out the front through the virtually empty parking lot. She then took off running as fast as her swollen and abused throat would allow down the sidewalk in the opposite direction she was supposed to go. As she rounded the corner, she saw a woman exiting one of Austin's yellow cabs in front of a group of office buildings halfway up the street. She increased her speed and managed to catch her just before she closed the cab door.

"Excuse me," Amber gasped, holding her hand across her neck in hopes of hiding any obvious damage, "but is this cab open now?"

"I suppose it is, yes," she replied, looking startled.

"Thanks!"

Amber popped her head into the back and asked the driver, "You accepting new fares?"

"Yeah. Hop in."

After climbing into the back seat, Amber made sure a thick lock of her hair looped across her neck. Her voice already sounded as though she had swallowed a bucketful of glass shards. She didn't want the driver to start asking uncomfortable questions.

"Where to?"

"Can you just drive around downtown for a few

minutes? I'm waiting for my friend to text me which bank I'm supposed to go to in that general area."

The man didn't even bat an eye at her unusual request. "No problem."

Amber clutched her phone tighter, trying to stop her hands from shaking. It really was a minor miracle that neither her phone nor sunglasses had been damaged during Garrett's assault.

By now, Raphek was probably beside himself because she never showed to meet him. She desperately wanted to call him to alleviate his worry, but now wasn't the time. His search for her had already likely begun. There were three dragon-men with noses better than a bloodhound's and ears that could hear a pin drop a mile away. Raphek had told her that it was harder to parse out individual voices depending on crowd size. Going to the heart of a city of nearly a million people should buy her a lot of time.

Thank God Otaron had given her a few twenties just in case she ran into any unforeseen snags while alone. He had given the same to Raphek, so she needed to confuse her scent trail as much as possible until six o'clock rolled around. Being able to take his own taxi or rideshare while Otaron also drove around lessened the effectiveness of her attempt to confuse her trail considerably.

Amber spent her time in the cab looking at pictures online of the park Garrett had designated as their meeting place. It looked to be a park full of trails surrounded by tons of trees and just off a lake. Fantastic. He had picked a place that was perfect for hiding a body.

But that was before you told him about the audio file proving his abuse.

Things could no doubt head south in a hurry this evening, but as long as the bastard believed that he could beat Matty's location out of her, he had an incentive not to kill her. Concerning the hinted doctored video and her audio file, that put them at a stalemate.

Hopefully, that'll be enough to keep Matty safe, to keep the firedrakes' hard-earned reputation safe. To keep Raphek safe...

Amber's hands were still shaking when she signaled for the cab driver to drop her off in front of the first bank that caught her eye. It was only then that she wondered if she were suffering from a mild case of shock. She should probably find a place to at least get a soda or something.

But first thing's first.

The bank she had chosen was just a satellite branch of a larger whole, small and thankfully with only a handful of people inside. She made a beeline for the bathroom, and once Amber determined that it was currently empty, she locked herself into a stall at the very end. She sagged against the stall door, and with her heart in her throat, she selected Raphek's burner phone's number from her contacts.

He picked up before the first ring could finish.

"Amber! I've been going mad looking for you! Are you all right? Did that piece of Terran scum—where are you, dearheart?" Raphek demanded all in one breath.

The endearment nearly broke her resolve.

"Raph, you had to have heard what went down," Amber said thickly. *Keep it together, dammit!* "That monster won't give up until he thinks he's won. Matty and I are just *things* to him. Trophies to prop up his political image. He doesn't give a damn if his father burns down the entire world to give him that win, even if the senator is doing it more to protect his own financial interests rather than his son's reputation. I'll be damned before I ever let either of them near Matty again or to drag the Draknos's good character through the mud."

Ugh! Her voice because of the near strangulation sounded worse and worse with every word. No doubt it was driving Raphek to distraction, and that's the last thing either one of them needed right now.

Nevertheless, Amber plowed on, "That's why I'm

going to meet him at the park at six and let him take me back to Houston."

"No."

That one word echoed in her mind and seemed to seep into her very soul like a warm embrace. Amber's legs nearly gave out. What was this? More dragon magic? There was more power in that one spoken syllable than Amber had ever heard in her life.

"I have to," she forced out. "For Matty. For *you*."

"When dragon-shifters fall in love," he said quietly, "they fall fast and hard. It's just our nature for our souls, what we call our Dragon Fire, to flare up with our most powerful emotions and continue to burn bright without end, especially for what we treasure. You and Matty are what I now treasure most, the ones my Fire burns hottest for within the core of my being. Thus, I'll see myself dead first before I will allow that creature that is an affront to all Terrans to extinguish the fire that was awakened within you both just in the short time we have spent together."

Amber closed her eyes tightly, unable to speak for fear that she would begin to sob.

The universe was certainly playing a cruel joke on her.

"Then for the first time in my life, I picked the right person to love," she said, her voice hitching.

Slowly, she placed a hand on her belly. What if? Would fate really punish her a second time with another pregnancy at the worst possible time? With a child, she realized in that moment, that she very much wanted to have with him, her kind and passionate dragon-man.

Yes, a cruel joke.

"Everything I'll have to endure from now on will be worth it," Amber forced herself to continue, "because I'll know that Matty is being cared for by a man like you who loves him. I'll find a way back to you and Matty. Somehow. Someday. I swear it. It just can't be today. Too many lives depend on me doing the right thing here because Raph, I couldn't live with their blood on my hands—or to force their blood to coat yours because you wanted to protect me."

Then Amber did one of the hardest things she had ever had to do. She hit the button to end the call.

She was about ten second from collapsing to the floor in a blubbering mess, but that was *not* a release she could afford right now. The clock was ticking, faster than even before because she knew damn well that Raphek wasn't just going to roll over and do what she asked. Not after *that* love confession.

With a sick feeling, Amber tapped in a number she had hoped to never call again.

"I'll meet you," Amber said without preamble as soon

as the line was picked up, "but not at Emma Long. Pick a park, any other park, and I'll meet you in an hour. Just me. Just you. That's the deal. Take it or leave it."

For a long while, there was nothing but silence from his end. No background chatter, no sounds of traffic, or even breathing. As the seconds ticked by, Amber began to fear that the bastard was just going to hang up on her without a word.

"Walnut Creek Metropolitan Park. The playground." The call then ended.

Garrett's voice had been tinged with amusement, and that scared Amber more than his rage ever had.

CHAPTER TWENTY-TWO

As Amber slowly approached the playground area of the park, she could see Garrett standing between two different sets of slides near... Her heart wrenched painfully. Near a purple dinosaur that kids could sit on. That couldn't be a coincidence, the utter bastard.

Amber was relieved to see that at least there were no children present. She wouldn't have put it past him to somehow use them against her. No other people nearby, either. She wasn't sure yet whether that was a good thing or a bad thing.

"You actually showed. Will wonders never cease," Garrett sneered once she was within earshot.

Amber stopped with about five feet still between them. "I had to make sure that you weren't going to do something incredibly stupid even after everything I told you," she replied frostily, though her tone was somewhat ruined by how hoarse her voice sounded.

His eyes narrowed. "We're only here now because *you're* the one who did something stupid. All you had to do was keep your mouth shut and do as you were told. That's what a good wife is *supposed* to do, but I suppose a dumb bitch like you is too dumb for even something as simple as that."

If someone would have told her this morning that Garrett was a pod person who had been replaced the day after their marriage, she wouldn't have thought them crazy at all. She couldn't for the life of her fathom how that charming, handsome young man she had met at a party after a college football game and the man standing before her with such a contemptuous expression were the same man.

Garrett Johnson was a complete sociopath, just like his father, and she hadn't seen the truth of it until it was far too late. She wondered if anyone else had ever seen the true monster behind the charm and what he had done to them to keep his dark secret.

"I think you have this century confused with the Dark Ages," Amber retorted. "I came here to try to talk some sense into you, to try to resolve this mess between us like two mature adults, but if you're just going to attack me with childish insults—"

Amber gasped when she suddenly found herself staring down the barrel of a gun.

"There's nothing to discuss," Garrett said sharply, the gleam in his eyes making Amber wonder with horror if he had lost it completely. "You're going to take a little walk with me along the trails here, and then you're going to call the asshole I know you've been spreading your legs for and tell him to bring Matthew here."

Amber had looked at photos of this park online, too. Many of the pictures taken along some of the trails had looked isolated and foreboding. There had also been some taken around a creek that she could well imagine Garrett dumping her body to be well-hidden by the wild foliage and crevasses in the rock formations along its banks. If he got her alone on one of those trails, then she knew she would never emerge alive.

"I *told* you, if you kill me, then you'll never find Matty," Amber said slowly, willing her voice not to shake. To Garrett, that would be like blood in a tank full of sharks. "Everyone will also hear the audio file that proves you're a monster."

"Who said anything about killing you?" he said with a wide smile that chilled her to the bone. "You have plenty of kneecaps, hands, feet, and elbows for me to shoot without the threat of you bleeding out too quickly. One for every time you refuse to answer me." He waved his gun in the direction she knew the entrance to one of the trails lay. "Now start walking."

Amber didn't move a muscle. "You really are crazy if you think I'm going to go anywhere with you! *Think, Garrett!* Why can't you see that there's no way shooting and torturing me will end well for you? Someone will hear the gunshots. They'll hear my screams. With that many witnesses, even your daddy's money and the Johnson name won't be able to shield you from the consequences!"

"Someone's already seen you," a woman's voice abruptly called out somewhere behind her.

Amber whipped her head around and then cried out as her abused neck instantly erupted in a sharp pain that brought tears to her eyes. Even so, none of that was enough to distract her from the scene straight from her worst nightmare that had shockingly come into play.

"What the hell are you—*how* did you—!" Amber stammered in anguish.

Taylor Madden, her backstabbing and now ex-lawyer, stood several feet behind them near a stone building, her right hand clutching the hand of a very terrified looking Matty dressed in unfamiliar, but Terran clothes.

"I didn't tell you to come here, but..." The look on Garrett's face was so gleeful and triumphant that for a split-second, Amber thought getting shot would be worth it if she could just punch him right in the center of that face as hard as she could.

"No, you didn't," Madden said crossly, "but after the phone call I just received full of demands from Senator Johnson, I've decided I've had enough of this madness." The woman then turned a steely gaze onto Amber. "No amount of money you pay me is worth being constantly threatened. I won't hide him for you any longer. I refuse to deal with this crazy family any longer."

Huh? Hide Matty? What the hell was the witch even —wait. Those last couple of words...

Like a punch to the gut, Amber's white-hot panic melted into a shocked understanding that sent her mind into overdrive. Although her speech patterns and brusque alto had been spot on, Madden's words, especially the last two, had been spoken with a slight accent —and it wasn't her usual Texas twang.

A conversation surfaced in her mind from breakfast that morning.

"TOO BAD YOU *need to look like you for the cameras in your*

lawyer's office," Otaron said between bites of toast. "Then we wouldn't have to worry about the wrong people spotting you."

Amber frowned. "You mean like dye my hair black and wear brown-tinted contacts like you do?"

"Oh no. Nothing so permanent. You have the loveliest shade of golden hair that it would be a travesty to alter it."

Raphek's warning growl made both Otaron and Airon laugh.

"What he means is that in these types of situations where one needs to temporarily hide their appearance, a glamour is usually used to great effect," Raphek explained.

Amber's eyes widened. "A glamour as in a type of magic spell?"

He nodded. "An illusion created by magic."

"Magic as in what Lady Serie used to heal my calf?"

"No," Raphic replied. "Lady Serie is a healer. A practitioner of a different discipline is need for this. The English word for them is 'mage,' and all magic users among the Rekkan have at least one Mikkan ancestor."

"Like me," Otaron said with a grin. "My grandmother, though her blood runs fairly thin in me. Most high-level spells are beyond me. I can't, for example, create a physical illusion that can be touched, but glamours? Piece of cake."

"Can you show me?" Amber asked a bit diffidently.

"Something small, then," Otaron agreed. "A glamour as elaborate as making a person look like an entirely different *person takes more time than we have for a quick demon-stration."*

He then turned to Airon and raised both his hands to face-level. The same faint, blue glow Amber had seen come from Lady Serie's hands now surrounded Otaron's. He did an elaborate series of gestures while his eyes were hyper-focused on Airon's face. The air was also noticeably charged, putting her in mind of getting too near a live wire.

Then between one blink and the next, Airon's nose faded out of existence, replaced with a smooth patch of skin.

Amber laughed in both delight and a little bit of horror. "That's one of the most amazing things I have ever seen!"

THERE WAS no way Matty could be here.

The only way what Amber was seeing before her could be real was if Raphek had betrayed her. That was something that even her jaded mind couldn't believe. The Taylor Madden and Matty before her *had* to be the work of a glamour, and there was only one dragon she had met that had that good of an American accent to speak for her and could perform magic.

"Glad to see that at least one woman on this earth isn't as dumb as a rock," Garrett said. "Now, here's what we're going to do. If you want to stay breathing, then you will come back to Houston with me and our son without a fuss. Then my father will arrange a little press conference where you will admit to the good people of Houston that you and the man you are having an affair with conspired to steal Matthew away from his own father. Once the media and public finish eviscerating you, I will announce that I have filed for divorce and full custody of our son. After that, you can go drown in a puddle of piss for all I care."

She had no idea what the dragons' play was here, but for now, it was probably best to play along with Garrett.

Amber opened her mouth, false words of agreement on the tip of her tongue, but before she could utter a single syllable, Garrett jammed the gun against her forehead, making her flinch. "And if that fucking audio file ever sees the light of day, I'll make you watch me force that damned brat to eat a bullet before doing the same to you, you stupid bitch!"

Her heart was beating so fiercely with fear that it took her a moment to realize that the pounding she was hearing wasn't just the sound of her heart.

"Sir! Step away from the woman, and drop your weapon! Now!" A deep voice demanded behind her.

Amber acted instinctively. She dropped to the ground as though her legs had been cut out from under her in a desperate move to get out of the way of the bullet she just knew was about to be fired. She was still in the process of covering her head with her arms in a feeble attempt for protection when Garrett abruptly dropped to his knees beside her, the gun falling out of his suddenly shaking hands.

"You got it all wrong!" he cried as he brought his now empty hands up. "This is *her* gun. She threatened to shoot me, and I took it away! I was just protecting myself and my son!"

"Son? Do you see a kid here? Because I don't," Another male voice said derisively behind her.

Amber chanced a glance over her shoulder and saw three policemen and one policewoman all pointing their guns at them, their stances a hair-trigger away from violence.

"Over there! Over there!" Garrett shouted, pointing his finger frantically at—she blinked in astonishment—a dirty, huge stuffed teddy bear sitting on the ground in the exact same spot that the fake Taylor Madden and fake Matty had stood only a minute or two ago.

"Your son needs a bath, I think," One of the cops muttered while another ordered Garrett to lay face-down on the ground with his hands behind his back.

Amber expected him to start yelling "Do you know who I am?" or something of the like, but shockingly, he never once brought up his name or the senator. He just continued to shout about his innocence, that they should be arresting his bitch of a wife who had just tried to kill him, dammit!

For her part, Amber just sat completely still and silent where she had fallen, her eyes not even straying towards the gun, her hands raised to chest level and open. Only when Garrett was handcuffed and being shuffled away did the female and the final male cop approach her.

"I'm Officer Lewis, and this is my partner, Officer Torres," the policewoman introduced. "Are you hurt, Miss?"

Amber pointed at her throat. "He grabbed me around the neck before he pulled the gun on me."

This police report, like all the others, would be swept under the rug. It was best to just keep things simple. She had absolutely no idea what the dragons' endgame would have been before the sudden appearance of the Austin PD had thrown a wrench into everything, including her own plans, but given that her confrontation with Garrett had ended without any bloodshed, having someone call the cops had likely been the best outcome.

"Looks like he also smacked you hard across the cheek," Officer Torres said with narrowed eyes.

In all the chaos, Amber had completely forgotten

about the backhand. "He did."

"And he's your husband?" Officer Lewis asked.

"Soon to be ex," Amber said angrily as she accepted the hand up from Officer Torres. "This all started at my lawyer's office because he found out I was about to serve him with divorce papers. I agreed to meet him in this park because it was public but not public, if you get what I mean. I never expected him to pull a gun on me."

"We'll need you to come down to the station to give an official statement. Did you come here in your own vehicle or…?" Officer Lewis asked.

"I took a cab," she replied.

The officer nodded. "We'll give you a ride."

Amber felt her phone buzz twice in quick succession in her pocket. She debated for a split-second whether or not to answer it before pulling it from her pocket. There was only one person who was bound to text her while she was being interrogated by cops.

Tell them that you can call an old college friend to pick you up from the station. Then pretend to call. Be sure to delete this message.

Amber made a face as she shoved the phone back into her pocket. "Just spam."

CHAPTER TWENTY-THREE

It was only when Amber reached the police station that the department realized the full enormity of Garrett's and her identity.

Suddenly, her statement became a full-blown interrogation. After reiterating that she was *not* missing and revealing that she had already informed the Houston PD and the FBI of her status as well as her divorce intentions, Amber's stay at the police station stretched while her information was verified. That they now had Senator Johnson's son in custody on a potential attempted murder charge, the very senator who only two days earlier had pleaded in a nationally-televised news conference for information on the whereabouts of the woman who was now the victim of his son's alleged crime, complicated everything threefold.

Amber had no doubt that Senator Johnson had already been contacted, and a pack of lawyers were on their way to the station. For long, terrifying moments as she sat alone in a small interrogation room after they had finished taking her statement about the assault as well as asking her questions regarding the missing persons report that had been filed on Matty and her, Amber had been deathly afraid that the senator would suddenly play the old kidnapping accusation card.

That's why when an officer came into the room what seemed like an eternity later and told her that she was free to go, Amber immediately suspected a trap. Just as Ms. Madden had ultimately screwed her over, Amber had totally expected the Austin PD to sell her out to Henry. She also knew because of the text that Raphek and company were somewhere nearby listening to every word spoken within the station. The combination of all those variables had the potential to ignite her worst-case scenario, the scenario she had tried to sacrifice herself to Garrett to prevent.

Why, *why* had she agreed to make an in-person state-ment now? Why had the dragons let her? She should have just called a cab and had it drop her somewhere remote where she could have then called Raphek to pick her up. She could have been safely tucked away in the dragons' safehouse with Raphek until it was safe to fly back to Elysia South.

Instead, Amber was now on her way out of the station with the air of a prisoner heading for the gallows after having pretended to call her "college friend" for a ride. It was only when she stepped past the row of concrete barriers, that she noticed the blond guy heading towards her from the parking lot to her right. Her first reaction was a wash of terror as her mind immediately thought that it was Garrett hurrying towards her. Her second was to continue walking and trying to learn to breathe again as she didn't recognize the man at all.

"Good! I thought I was running a bit late," the blond said as he stopped right in her path.

Amber stiffened in alarm and then she gasped when she realized that the guy was dressed in the exact jeans and red polo shirt with the tiny black polo logo that Otaron had been wearing when he had dropped her off at the diner.

"Ollie..." she said uncertainly.

He nodded so imperceptibly that she would have missed it had she not been scrutinizing his face. The relief she felt almost brought her to her knees.

"Jeez, you look like you were in a car accident!" he

said with a frown. "Forget your hotel, you're staying with me for the night. No arguments."

She offered him a weary smile, hearing the very real chastisement buried in his words. "Whatever you think is best. I'm about to fall over."

Remembering what he had said about the fragility of glamours, Amber was careful not to touch him as she followed him to, not the car from that morning, but a black F-150 truck. They didn't speak again until they were several blocks away from the police station and heading south.

"Raphek's pissed isn't he?"

Otaron's eyes slanted briefly towards her. "Yes, but not at you."

Amber sagged in her seat. "I've really made a mess of things again. I thought for sure the cops would hand me over to Senator Johnson's 'custody,' but since that didn't happen, I have no idea what he'll do now that his son's been arrested for attempted murder. This trip was supposed to make all of us safer, but now I think we're worse off than before."

"Oh, he'll release a doctored video of the border incident," Otaron said matter-of-factly. "But he was always going to find a reason to do that, so you shouldn't feel one iota of guilt when it happens. We just need to prepare ourselves to counter whichever way he chooses to slander us. Now, see that stop sign up ahead next to all those large shrubs and trees? The second I stop, get out and walk to your right. Raphek is there waiting for you among the shrubbery. He and Airon will get you back to the safehouse. I'm going to lead any possible tails on a merry stroll around Austin for the next hour."

Works as "just the king's eyes and ears" her foot! With his uncanny ability to disguise himself as virtually anyone and all this sneaking around, this dragon-shifter was straight up Ethan Hunt from the *Mission Impossible* movie franchise!

"Thanks, Ollie," Amber said as she slipped out of the truck before it had come to a complete stop.

She was only able to take a few steps around the corner before she was abruptly grabbed around the middle and pulled between a couple of large flowering shrubs into someone's yard. Yet, she wasn't in the least alarmed because a familiar warmth had completely enveloped her, a warmth she had thought she might not ever get to bask in again.

"Raph!"

A hard kiss was her answer, one that didn't last nearly long enough.

"I'm going to roast that bastard alive!" Raphek growled, his eyes literally blazing with red fire as he ran a thumb gently over the entirety of her neck.

Yep. The bruises were as bad as she had feared.

"And when we get back to the safehouse," he continued in that same rumbling voice that seemed to vibrate up her spine and make her shiver in excitement, "I'm going to bury myself so deep into your heat and make the core of you burn with the most exquisite pleasure that you never again think to leave my arms out of sacrifice."

Amber buried her face into his chest. "I didn't want to."

"I know," Raphek murmured into her hair, "and that's what makes it worse, that you thought you had no other choice but to go anyway. Come. Airon's waiting to pick us up a few blocks down."

Soon after crossing through a series of yards and back alleys, they were slipping into the backseat of the silver car Otaron had driven that morning. Amber was almost shocked that they had made it this far without incident.

"All clear?" Airon asked as he pulled back onto the street.

"As far as I could tell," Raphek said as he hugged Amber closer to his side as though he thought she was in danger of being snatched from him right then and there.

"Same here." Amber saw Airon gaze back at them

from the rearview mirror and scowl. "We should have torn out the asshole's neck when we had the chance."

"Agreed," Raphek growled darkly.

Amber sighed and shook her head. "You know that would've just made things worse at the park."

"I meant before the park," Airon said.

Amber leaned forward. "So you *did* see him enter Ms. Madden's building!"

"No. He went in through the emergency exit in the back. He was already acting the asshole inside the lawyer's office by the time we realized what was happening. Raphek, of course, wanted to immediately go inside."

Raphek bared his teeth. "But they stopped me. For good reason, I admit—at least in the beginning. When I heard you gasping frantically for breath and your heartbeat skyrocket, nothing short of the destruction of this earth would have kept me out of that building."

"But I didn't see any of you, even when I left the building after Garrett left," Amber said.

"Garrett was already leaving the building by the time we made it to the back alley," Airon explained. "We thought it best to follow Garrett in the car while Raphek stayed behind to meet you as planned."

"Only, I made the mistake of thinking you were going to circle the building before heading to meet me,"

Raphek said with a grimace. "By the time I realized you weren't coming, you were long gone, and your scent stretched for miles along several different paths."

Amber winced guiltily. "I grabbed a cab and intentionally confused my scent trail by having the driver aimlessly drive around downtown before dropping me off at a bank. That's when I called you, Raph."

"Smart," Airon said. "In the meantime, while your lover there was ready to burn down the entirety of Austin to smoke you out, Otaron and I found the hotel lounge Garrett was downing drinks at and heard your conversation with him."

"I wondered how you had found us so quickly." She abruptly glared at Airon's reflection in the rearview mirror. "That illusion of Matty nearly gave me a heart attack!"

Raphek kissed her temple tenderly. "Sorry about that, dearheart, but we needed to give the bastard an incentive to incriminate himself. It was the best we could come up with in such a short amount of time."

"Incriminate? But—even if any of you saw him hurting me or threatening to hurt Matty, it's not as though you could testify as witnesses without blowing your covers!"

"I filmed the entire encounter with one of our burner phones," Raphek said. "I was perched on a rather thick tree branch in one of the trees behind one of those colorful children's amusements full of chutes and stairs."

Amber gasped. "How did I miss you? I was practically looking right at you the whole time!"

"Otaron hid me with a glamour that mimics the surrounding environment as long as I stayed fairly still," Raphek replied.

"And the teddy bear?"

"Again, Otaron's idea. Apparently, he had won it in a game while out with a group of young Terrans at some sort of festival. He needed something large for the glamour to work, as well as something that could be left behind without suspicion once the police showed up. We dirtied it up to make it look as though it had been out there for at least a few days, and then wearing the same type of glamour as Raphek, Otaron snuck up and cast the glamour at the most opportune moment. He, of course, also provided Madden's voice."

"Wait! *You* were the ones that called the police?"

"We called as soon as you arrived at the park," Raphek said. "We could smell that he had a gun. That fact provided the final piece of the story we wished to create. We anonymously reported a man threatening a young woman with a gun. That Garrett ended up making himself look even more the madman because of the teddy bear was just a fortuitous accident that I, of course, filmed."

"As soon as I edit it, I'll be leaking the footage onto the internet tonight," Airon added.

"You can't!" Amber cried. "That'll just make the senator counter it with the footage of Raph taking Matty and me into Elysia South!"

"He was going to do it anyway," Airon said with a sigh. "At least this way, it'll just look like tit for tat. People may be less inclined to believe the senator's narrative, especially for a senator known for anti-dragon rhetoric."

"How do you even know that phrase?" Amber groaned.

True to his word, the moment they reached the safe-house, Raphek picked Amber up into a bridal carry and practically flew up the stairs. She swore she heard Airon laughing behind them, but it was kind of hard to hear anything over the pounding of her heart that sounded as loud as drums in her ears.

"I hate that I can hear the violence that bastard did to you in your voice," Raphek said as they entered the room they had shared last night.

Amber planted a soft, affectionate kiss to the side of his neck. "Then make me forget, the pain, the fear, every night until I can scream your name clearly again."

Amber's laugh when Raphek tumbled them both to the bed may have been a bit broken and hoarse, but she could still hear the joy she felt being in Raphek's arms again in it. Raphek found her lips parted and eager. Damn but this man could kiss. The way he alternated between sucking hard and then drawing back to slowly tease with the softest caress of his lips followed by the slick caress of his tongue against hers soon had Amber moaning and wrapping her legs around his waist. She squeezed her thighs against his sides in a silent plea to relieve the throbbing in her core his kisses had ignited.

She groaned in protest as Raphek pulled away and began to undress them both. "I can't go slowly right now," he growled once he had her nude and was pushing a muscled thigh between her legs to part them. "I must bury myself deep within you now or else I fear I'll go mad with want. Later, I will slowly taste and worship your body all night until your mind is consumed completely with pleasure, I promise."

Amber reached up and pulled him down for a hard kiss that had her panting when they parted. "Take me," she moaned. "Make me really feel it."

A couple of scorching hot fingers reached down between her legs as he passionately took her lips again and began to massage rough circles over her clit, making her wet in preparation for his monster of a cock. Amber bucked and writhed against that rough, sensual touch until she tore her mouth from his and begged him to fill her with a voice that was nearly gone.

Instantly, the fingers seemingly disappeared and were replaced with an even silkier, thicker heat. Amber dug her nails into her lover's shoulder with a cry as he thrust the head of his cock into her passage. His cock felt just as big and delicious as the first time as he slid it home with a second, harder thrust that made her cry out his name.

His hips started up a deep, circular dance as he buried himself over and over into her heat, his thrusts hard, stretching and stroking her in all those places within her passage that Amber had never known could send such toe-curling thrills of pleasure throughout her body. She had never known that being filled so completely could feel like *this*.

Something warm, yet hard kept flittering against her fingertips as she gripped his back, and it was only when she opened her eyes as she gasped for breath between kisses that Amber realized what she was feeling was his red and black scales starting to manifest in chaotic patterns all over his body as well as rippling like waves across his face.

Combined with the vertical slits of his dragon eyes, it should have been a frightening visage, but Amber only felt awe that this beautiful, powerful, and majestic being was finding so much pleasure wrapped in her arms and buried deep within her that he was so very obviously losing control.

"I love you," Amber whispered against his lips.

Raphek's entire body tightened a split-second before his lips crashed onto her own, devouring her in a kind of wild abandon even as his hips began to thrust into her with an equal wild intensity that was at the brink of being too much for her to handle but at the same time, oh so perfect.

When the pleasure building in her sex exploded, she literally saw white behind her closed eyelids, her orgasm made all the more intense by Raphek's unrelenting thrusts. Her lover swallowed those cries too, seemingly a catalyst to add even more speed to his hips that inadvertently caused her to squeeze her inner muscles around his cock.

It was Raphek's turn to moan deeply as his once steady rhythm fell apart as he began to climax. Just as before, a flood of molten seed filled her passage, and she cried out Raphek's name. It was a sensation she was sure she would never fully get used to but at the same time, was coming to appreciate the uniqueness it brought to an already mind-blowing experience.

Raphek continued to heavily thrust into her as he

orgasmed, and Amber wrapped herself even more tightly around him in every way, his thrusts still enhancing the remaining echoes of her own climax she vocalized as soft sighs.

When his hips finally stilled, Raphek allowed himself to just lay upon her with a little bit more of his weight than before for a few blissful moments. The weight of him pressing her down into the mattress was nice and not suffocating at all. It was a peaceful moment of connection that soothed her wounded soul in a way she hadn't thought was possible.

A few minutes later, he carefully withdrew from her with a contented sigh and rolled them until she was lying half-draped over him, legs entangled. For a few minutes more, they were both content to just cuddle in silence.

As Raphek lazily ran one of his hands through her long locks, Amber knew that she had to ask the one question that had once nearly sent her into a panic attack but now represented a future she very much wanted. "I know that it's *way* too late to be asking you this," Amber said, "but is it possible that I may have gotten pregnant?"

"Would that please you?" he asked, his hand never once pausing in its stroking.

His question threw her for a loop. Amber had half-expected him to stiffen or even to just give her a simple yes or no in his usual blunt way. She hadn't expected him to treat her question as if it were a completely normal discussion for them to have and not in the "Oh my God, we forgot to use protection!" kind of way.

"When I remembered that I missed several doses of my birth control pills, I have to admit I panicked. Unplanned pregnancies always complicate things with very few exceptions. An unplanned pregnancy was how I ended up married to Garrett. While I will never regret having Matty, I was pretty mad at myself that I never once thought about the possibility of me getting pregnant as we were having sex. But then, as I stood in a bathroom stall after I had told you that I had to go back to Garrett to protect us all, I remembered that I could be pregnant again, and I realized that I really wanted that potential baby—because it was *yours*."

Amber felt Raphek's breath hitch beneath her cheek.

"Then we'll create that baby together," he said gruffly. He tightened the arm around her waist. "Someday, when you are truly ready, and most importantly, when you are truly ready to accept a piece of my Dragon Fire. We must Bond as mates first before a child is possible between us, and Draknos mate for eternity—literally."

Amber lifted her head up and saw the truth in his eyes. "Draknos are…immortal?

"Yes. For the Rekkan, as long as our Dragon Fire is not extinguished, we will never die."

Eternity really wasn't something she could wrap her head around. That was something she would have to think long and hard about when her mind wasn't one step away from complete mush because her apparently immortal lover had just screwed her brains out.

"You told me earlier that your Dragon Fire was like your soul…"

Raphek released his hold on her waist. "If you will move away from my chest for a moment, I will show you my Dragon Fire."

Amber rolled over and then pushed herself into a seated position, curious but apprehensive at the same time. Just what kind of marvel was she about to see?

Raphek cupped the air with both hands over the middle of his chest, and between one breath and the next, a red glow, hot and bright, rose from within his chest into his hands. Amber gasped. It was literally a sphere of raging red fire, dancing and pulsating with heat and life. She could feel the heat of it on her bare skin as though she were sitting near a furnace.

"That has to be one of the most beautiful things I've ever seen," she gushed.

Raphek allowed it to sink back into his chest. "That's why courtships and mating bonds are so very sacred to my people. I will literally be giving you a piece of my soul should we decide to mate. You would share my life-span as well because of that sacred connection."

Amber stared at him, suddenly so overwhelmed by what she was hearing that she didn't know what to say or even what she should be feeling. Raphek smiled and curled an arm around her again, urging her to lay across his chest again, which she did almost in a daze. He kissed the top of her head and then resumed running his fingers through her hair.

"Raph…"

"I know," he said, kissing her head again. "We are still very early into our courting, and that was a topic for another day far down the line. Matty must also play a very integral part to that discussion. We'll revisit it when you feel that day has come. For now, rest a bit, sleep, and when you wake, I'll begin my worship of your body, beginning with my mouth."

Amber shivered. "And after your mouth has had its fill of my body, then—maybe I can taste yours?"

She reached a hand down and circled his member with her fingers, giving it a gentle squeeze.

Red fire flashed in his eyes.

"Most definitely."

EPILOGUE

"...*And to the person who released an unaltered video over social media of the dragon saving my life and my son's life on that terrible day, words aren't enough to thank you. It sickened me when I saw how all the anti-dragon groups were spreading the lie of the first, heavily doctored video of us that popped up. That Senator Johnson was also trying to use that doctored video as proof that the Draknos were to blame for my ex-husband's crimes against me and our son sickened me. I'm sure everyone saw that particular damning video of Garrett when it leaked. Garrett Johnson was enough of a recognizable type of monster—and unfortunately, a common one in human society—without anyone having to explain his behavior away with an absurd conspiracy theory about the Draknos messing with men's minds so they can steal their women and*

children. That said, because my son and I are still being used to further the agendas of those hate groups even after that first video was thoroughly debunked is why I agreed to this interview..."

"Ugh, please stop watching that, Raph," Amber moaned as she walked into the main room of their home. "You've only been home from patrolling for thirty minutes, tops!"

"But I love how your eyes were so fierce as you defended me," Raphek said with a completely serious look.

"It's embarrassing is what it is," she insisted as she plopped herself down on the couch so she could snuggle next to him. "I only did that stupid interview so that we could wash our hands of Garrett and his damn father for good. Frankly, I'm shocked that the masses sided with us."

"The president being on our side was a big part of that," Raphek said pointedly.

Amber snorted. "That's only because King Dagon ripped her a new one about how she was allowing Senator Johnson and his ilk to slander the Draknos day after day without consequence—and you're *still* watching!"

"Fine. For you," Raphek said, pausing the video and then pressing a soft kiss to her lips that immediately heated her blood. "How are your Draknar lessons going?"

Amber made a face. "Can you believe that Matty can speak it better than me?"

Raphek laughed. "Children simply absorb things better. That's all."

"Matty also plays practically every day with Sabon, so I'm sure they're both picking up each other's language faster because of it."

"Is that where he is now?"

Amber nodded. "He should be home any minute now since it's almost dinnertime."

"He's just excited that he'll 'be able to talk like a dragon to grandma and grandpa' when your parents visit in a couple of weeks."

Amber laughed. "He said that?"

"He also said that he wanted us to get a mog to show your parents, too," Raphek warned.

Amber winced. "He's not going to give up, is he?"

"Considering how much he loves Jaws and his friend has two..."

"Dammit. My parents are nervous enough coming to a place with nothing but dragon-shifters as it is. Imagine having to deal with the lovechild of Dolly and Jaws wanting a lot of petting."

"Who's Dolly?"

Before Amber could answer, the front door swung open, and Matty practically came flying into the room. Amber barely moved the tablet out of Raphek's lap in time before Matty all but tackled him. "Daddy! Sabby's mog is gonna have babies! He said I can have one!"

Amber froze. Did Matty just call Raphek…

She suddenly didn't care that Sabon's mother was there to witness. She promptly burst into tears of joy.

And now there was no way Matty wasn't going to get a baby mog.

…and maybe a baby sister or brother.

ABOUT THE AUTHOR

Cristina Rayne is a *New York Times* and *USA Today* best-selling author who lives in West-Central Texas with her crazy cat and about a dozen bookcases full of fantasy worlds and steamy romances. She has a degree in Computer Science which totally qualifies her to write romances. As Fantasy is her first love, she feels if she can inject a little love into the fantastical, along with a few steamy scenes, then all the better. She is the author of the *Elven King, The Elven Realms, Riverford Shifters, Dragon Shifters of Elysia, Incarnations of Myth, Lords of the Vampire Underground* paranormal romance series, and the *Fractured Multiverse* science-fantasy series.

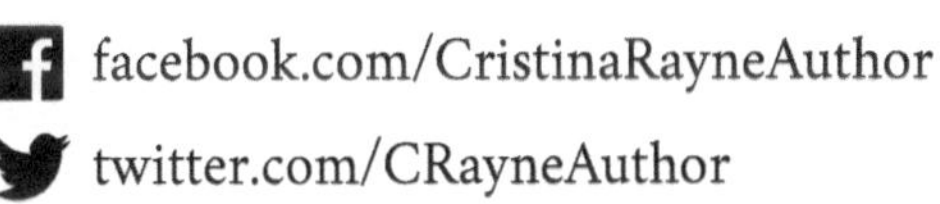

facebook.com/CristinaRayneAuthor

twitter.com/CRayneAuthor